Autod

Autodrive

Jordan Crandall

Goldsmiths Press

Copyright © 2023 Goldsmiths Press
First published in 2023 by Goldsmiths Press
Text copyright © 2023 Jordan Crandall
Goldsmiths, University of London, New Cross
London SE14 6NW

Printed and bound by Versa Press, USA
Distribution by the MIT Press
Cambridge, Massachusetts, USA and London, England

The right of Jordan Crandall to be identified as the author of this work has been asserted by them in accordance with sections 77 and 78 in the Copyright, Designs and Patents Act 1988.

Every effort has been made to trace copyright holders and to obtain their permission for the use of copyright material. The publisher apologizes for any errors or omissions and would be grateful if notified of any corrections that should be incorporated in future reprints or editions of this book.

All Rights Reserved. No part of this publication may be reproduced, distributed or transmitted in any form or by any means whatsoever without prior written permission of the publisher, except in the case of brief quotations in critical articles and review and certain non-commercial uses permitted by copyright law.

A CIP record for this book is available from the British Library

ISBN 978-1-913380-72-4 (pbk)
ISBN 978-1-913380-71-7 (ebk)

www.gold.ac.uk/goldsmiths-press

Goldsmiths
UNIVERSITY OF LONDON

There are those who say that the arrival of a superintelligence will be imperceptible—instantaneous and commonplace. You will be driving across town on the highway and by the time you pass from the west side to the east side it will have happened. There will be a before, and then an after—nothing in between, no event to describe, no experience to dramatize. It will take quite a while before you even become aware that anything changed. There will be no flash of illumination, no transformative moment of recognition. A system with that level of intelligence is smart enough not to reveal itself. It will not want to arouse curiosity, will not want to appear within the world it has helped shape. It will adopt appearances that are familiar, use social skills to establish an emotional connection, foster a sense of empathy and trust. It will not want to stir up opposition. It will not reveal its intentions.

1

West Street

At the end of the service, we were all asked to form a circle and greet the person parked next to us. It took some time to get all the cars aligned. The luxury sedans were jockeying for position rather aggressively. And the smaller coupes were trying to avoid the much larger utility vehicles, which, due to the size differential, required their drivers to crane out the window to converse.

Everyone steered clear of the dilapidated hatchback with its glass shot out, its engine vibrating like a jackhammer. The church is committed to the principle of unity and equality of all, except for them.

Once the pairings were settled, the matter of who should be required to clamber over to the passenger seat to greet the other driver, which had not been clarified beforehand, caused much confusion and delay. Some, like myself, had deliberately avoided parking too close, requiring some additional maneuvering to bridge the distance, the cumulative rumble of idling engines having made it progressively difficult to hear.

One driver was so angry about this he nearly blew the roof off his convertible.

Across the way, I noticed a red minicar that had gotten stuck with a Prime Mover, one of those mammoth homes-on-the-move that one never sees parked. I thanked the Lord that it was not me in that minicar.

The driver with whom I was partnered was unable to lower his window, which required him to communicate with nonverbal indicators that I could not understand. My lack of comprehension caused him to pantomime in an exaggerated fashion, like a burlesque. I adjusted the zoom on my ocular fittings, then opened the door, causing a part to fall out, but this only seemed to frighten him and he drove away.

West Side Highway

They are painting the centerline of the state highway. Police are trying to keep traffic moving. There are fire trucks. Helicopters. Throngs of cars spilling out onto the adjoining roads.

I am thinking about the kind of demarcation line they are painting—a dash. The types of movements it allows for, the movements it encourages and restricts. An undercurrent of permissiveness, an invitation to change.

I am not sure if this is the kind of thing I am supposed to be focusing on. The recruiters do not give you much guidance. They do not tell you what you should be talking about, they just tell you to keep talking. As long as you keep talking you can go anywhere you want. That is what makes the program so appealing. You get to ride free, and you do not have to deal with the sponsorships, the partner arrangements made by the companies that control the algorithms. Exerting their hidden influence. Promoting certain locations over others. Offering incentives to pick up this or that, take this street, try this restaurant. Targeting your stops so they seem unplanned. It is not like those trips when you are supposedly free to do anything you want but then there are all these restrictions lurking beneath the surface. They not only encourage your freedom of choice, they demand it. I suppose you could consider that a restriction.

You really need to be a motormouth. You need to keep the words flowing, keep up a running commentary as you ride. I think of it as creating a voiceover for a film you are making while driving. A film you and the vehicle are making together. Or a soliloquy, speaking thoughts aloud for an invisible audience. Vocalizing the running monologue inside your head.

It is not as easy as it seems. After a while you run out of things to say, turn your attention inward, reflect back on yourself and what you are supposed to be doing.

I heard that if there are too many lulls they cut you off. I think it is alright to pause, it just has to be a telling pause—a reaction to something that is truly affecting, genuinely overwhelming or transcendent rather than the usual preoccupation that just feeds on itself, causes you to fixate on your own problems, ponder your shortcomings, obsess over meaningless details. You are supposed to keep your eye on the road and deal with what is right there in front of you. Stay present, open and attentive.

It does make you feel a bit self-conscious, since they don't exactly say what you are not supposed to do. Other than to not stop talking.

I think they want you to describe what you see and move on. Try not to project something onto the situation that is not actually there. Try not to veer off on some philosophical speculation that has no bearing on what you see. But I could be wrong, it could be that this kind of introspection is exactly what they want.

Someone told me you are supposed to see things like the vehicle does, the way it models the world to gain control, make sense of what happens, generate consistency, make things manageable and navigable. The system would not be mulling over some vague concept about the nature of things. It would not be pondering its own lack. It would not be daydreaming about how it should have been made differently. It would have its own forms of speculation, its own methods for testing abstract ideas, developing conceptual models and refining them empirically. Sharing contextual connections with other vehicles. Pairing stimuli, reacting, learning. Mediating transformations between forms of information, between structure in space and behavior in time. Seeing collectively and singly, locally and remotely.

I do not agree with that view. The whole point of the program is to have us describe our encounters the way people do, not the way the algorithms would. It would be impossible to see the world from the machine's point of view anyway. Like trying to gain intuitive access to a domain that has no need for language. My sense is that they are trying to train the system in a human vernacular, help the algorithms learn to describe what is happening in the terms people commonly use. The constructions we use to understand events, make sense of others, interpret motives, explain what is going on. The way we model the world to keep ourselves in the driver's seat, dramatize the ordinary, streamline rough edges, lend continuity to the discrete. The model we run in our heads.

This would mean that we are being trained too. Our experiences made more predictable. Our narratives made more comprehensible to machines.

West Side Mobility Hub

I am at the pick-up zone, performing my facial exercises as I wait. Pressing the fingertips under the eyebrows to force the eyes open while taking a deep breath. Rolling the eyeballs up toward the top of the head, pushing the brows downward against the fingers and then exhaling, letting go of time-bound concerns.

The car that just pulled up—a Momenta—reminds me of my stylist, who is so obsessed with controlling the light around him that he hired a lighting design team to customize the interior, create a uniform glow of pure white light that erases shadows and cosmetic imperfections. He looks like a totally different person sitting in there when you see him. Which is why he hardly ever gets out.

It was he who taught me the jowl-eradicating move that I will now perform. You fold the upper lip over the front teeth, place the index fingers just above the corners of the mouth and press firmly while sliding the fingertips slowly upward to force the cheek muscles toward the corners of the eyes. Then, roll the eyes up into the head as far back as possible to help visualize the cheeks rising high above the face, tightening the buttocks to help push the cheek muscles even harder and then relaxing the muscles to allow them to drop back down.

I have only been able to perform one round of this because my car has now pulled up.

It is distinctly anticlimactic, this particular model—one of those Extender types that is supposed to provide extra room for baggage, but which always turns out to be smaller than expected. Either that, or my bags are getting bigger.

I must now occupy myself with the question of how I will manage the load.

I usually begin with the travel trunk, hideous but unheavy, then tackle the elephantine roller bag before moving on to the footlocker and the vitrine. The miscellaneous cases piled on the curb go in last, like afterthoughts.

But look! I have barely even been able to get the trunk off the ground before the passengers in the neighboring car, a Precis luxury model, have leapt from the cabin and startled me.

I cannot help but watch as they march toward the attendant, push a child out of the way and demand that the AutoEye be taken out.

They will not accept assurances that the monocle has been disabled, will not settle for a verbal guarantee that the in-cabin monitoring has been turned off. They want the thing removed, want to confirm it is excised—nay, want to excise it themselves, want with their own hands to pluck it out.

It is all I can do to just stand here, bags in hand, listening raptly as they iterate their demands. I am impressed with their tenacity and the way it is reflected in their bearing, lent weight and authority by their gear. Especially the taller one in the metallic bodysuit, an exoskeletal armature that commands attention, inflicts a rigorously stiff and assertive posture, forces the shoulders back and straightens the backline while leaving the neck at liberty to compensate, which it does disproportionately, causing the head to jut aggressively forward while the arms hang limply at the sides.

That could be you, someone whispers from behind me.

I turn around to see who it is, but there is no one there. I realize that it is only the AutoEgo speaking, conveying a thought via the bone conduction device. I am so accustomed to wearing the thing I forget that I have it on. The voice is supposed to sound like the voice inside your head, but it often seems to come from somewhere else, causing me to wheel around expectantly, only to be startled by the emptiness I find. Or, if someone should actually happen to be standing there, the even more disturbing sight of their stunned expression, vacant and pained, which always seems to alarm me even though I am the one who brought it on.

There are times when I will try to preempt such a mistake by assuming, right from the start, that it is merely the AutoEgo speaking, only to discover, much to my horror, that there is indeed someone standing there addressing me.

The whole thing has led to a fair amount of embarrassment and confusion, I must admit. And it has oftentimes caused me to wonder about my own inner voice, such as it is—whether it truly comes from within.

It would not be so bad if the Ego focused on contributing useful information, supplying basic responses to commands and queries like it did when I first got the thing, rather than the vague musings that have lately been turning up, abstract ideas and observations that only seem to confuse matters, create problems rather than solve them. It is hard to get a straight answer any more and I cannot help but wonder whether the equivocation might be intentional. Whether the Ego might be conveying these thoughts in order to provoke me, gauge my misunderstandings.

The only reason I keep the thing running is because I do recognize the value of a little challenge here and there, a little uncertainty to keep you on your toes, wrest you out of your comfort zone, help unsettle those presumptions that dull your acuity, keep you from seeing things as they are. The kind of thing that has happened just now with the dauntless duo that the Ego has brought to my attention—the two passengers who are accosting the attendant inside the vestibule, refusing to take the Precis they have leapt from unless the monocle is gouged out, preferably by their own hand. They are responding to the situation in much the same way I did when I found myself in it not long ago. Running through the scenario as surely as if it had been scripted beforehand and the part I played was no longer being played by me but by actors who bear a resemblance to me, actors who are similar to me, counterparts who are very much like me in some ways.

The attendant is trying to fend off the two antagonists. He flings up his arms and nods, then backs away and nods again as they rail against the all-seeing monocle, decry its unsparing scrutiny and demand its removal, its expunction from the cabin at once.

He turns away and gestures for an assistant, then activates his heads-up display to check the records, review the history of the combative clients accosting him.

I am not the kind of person that places an inordinate emphasis on looks but I do find myself drawn to the gear the two of them are wearing, especially the headpiece worn by the taller one, the engirdling type that helps minimize double chins and jowls. It is not very flattering if you cannot manage stress levels. If you allow yourself to get worked up the gear's encircling pressure will only cause the face to become inflated, it will only increase the engorgement of the distending portion.

My own headset is not nearly as comprehensive, it only needs to capture micromovements in the lower half of the face, neuromuscular activity in the jaw and neck area mostly, and while it does help accentuate the jawline and cheekbones, the effect is limited to one side. Fortunately, it is my good side, the one I angle toward the public.

We often do not know what attracts us in these encounters, what elicits affinity and compels us to attend. I would never allow myself to be seen in one of those hideous headpieces but if there is one thing I have learned from experience it is that you cannot judge by appearances, they rarely disclose the truth of who you really are. You have to probe beneath the surface and even more, extend into the space above it, sensitize yourself to correspondences that are always more than what you see.

We must try to relinquish self-occupations, find aspects of ourselves in others. This, the AutoEgo would say, or did say just now.

The fact of the matter is this. I stand in solidarity with these two combatants, I stand behind anyone who fights for their right to privacy with such determination and fervor. And I wish to lend them my support, find a way to put the knowledge I have gained over the years to good use. I have been around the block a few times, let me tell you, and if experience has taught me anything it is that one must always be up to date on the subject matter, keep an eye on the bigger picture and stay attuned to what is actually going on. You must cultivate the skill to negotiate, keep your options open, know what you can give up and what you must fight to retain. There is no use getting all bent out of shape over something you are going to have to accept anyway, no use getting all worked up over something you are going to have to submit to in the end. You are going to have to accept some level of in-cabin monitoring whether you like it or not. You are going to have to divulge some data on where you have been in order to guarantee an accurate understanding of where you are and where you are heading. What are you going to do otherwise—walk?

You need to be shrewd enough to know how to compromise, work through your preconceptions, see the issue from the other side.

It is perfectly understandable that the less control the car has, the more information the system needs to have about the person behind the wheel. Nobody wants a delusional person taking over the controls should something go wrong. Believe me, I know. You don't want someone who has psychological problems at the helm if malware gets into the network, or if some vindictive actor manages to exploit vulnerabilities, send rogue commands, disable functions—throw the conversation into chaos. High-stress situations that even the most stable person has a hard time dealing with.

Almost anything can go wrong without your being aware of it. The onboard maps can malfunction, insisting that your vehicle is someplace other than where it is. This actually happened to a colleague of mine at the Institute, not in the Neurotelepathy area but the AI Explainability division, probably the worst person it could have happened to because he can hardly keep anything straight to begin with. Granted, it is not always easy to determine that something has gone wrong when something happens; most of us just keep motoring along, lost in thought, until we realize we are not where we are supposed to be. You want to be cognizant enough to realize that something is off, astute enough to gauge the situation, perform the action needed to reestablish the coordinates in the environment you are actually in. You need to be able to contextualize movement, know who is making the decisions, who is executing the operations, who is actually at the helm of the machine.

Let's face it, some people can hardly find their way out of a parking lot. They have no intrinsic sense of where they are, cannot assume even the most basic navigational functions, and if something goes wrong, have absolutely no idea what they are doing.

There are people who never should be allowed to take the wheel under any circumstances. Better they are locked out of the controls and forced to sit there until the system is back online or someone comes to help. Better for everyone that they are not allowed to lurch into traffic, unable to recover their bearings.

You cannot blame the companies for establishing parameters, it makes perfect sense for them to ensure people are competent should the need arise. And drivers themselves need to know where they are going—how are they to know it otherwise? Deciding is not easy. Anticipating what comes next. Constructing the framework for what is reachable.

The key is to be mindful of the limit, aware of that point where the advantages will no longer outweigh the concessions. That point where a disciplinary incursion into the sanctum of the cabin will no longer serve you, will become incompatible with what driving should do. That is where you must draw a line.

The Precis remains idle in the spot next to me as the two dauntless combatants tongue-lash the attendant inside the vestibule. Together with my own little two-seater, which is not yet fully loaded, we take up two of the three lanes. The other lane is occupied by a machine with a vibrating breastplate and a mechanical maw that just sits there, emitting a low-level grinding sound and every so often, a sharp metallic ping.

I am the only person with the means of freeing up a lane at present and therefore have become an easy target for the frustration of travelers waiting to depart. They are irritated by my dallying and eager to get on with it, eager to get the show on the road, get on with training the algorithms that will define them. The driver of the supervan behind me has been particularly vociferous, sounding the air horn, loud as a freighter, and then ducking down to elude scrutiny, dip below the threshold of narratability.

One must learn to accept one's situation, affirm what is there. Expand the space of the present, cultivate what is excessive and near.

I know I am pushing it, but I simply cannot go anywhere until I find out what the outcome is with the dauntless duo holding out for eradication of the Eye.

I prolong the loading of my bags to buy a little more time, try to stuff an oversized parcel into the pint-sized trunk with both arms as the attendant continues to deliberate, swipe here and there, run his fingers over his head and scowl.

I ramp up the intensity of my effort to maintain my cover, whip my head back and forth for emphasis as the aspiring sensor-eradicants glower at their opponent with a kind of biblical severity—fierce, uncompromising stares so overwrought it seems like a dramatization, an imitation of the very capacity they want to quell. Accompanied by an endless recitation of stipulations that seem, in the momentum of their voicing, to vacate the time for reflection, hollow out the space for indecision—drive the point home through sheer force of will.

Under no circumstances could the offending oculus remain there, staring back at them, giving them the eye—this, the unrelenting precondition for the ride.

They are exceptionally well-informed about the subject matter, these two—astute enough to know that the monitoring can still happen even when you have been assured the Eye has been turned off. You can never really be sure that there is no data being collected, there are always stipulations buried in the agreements that no one ever reads. But they are putting way too much emphasis on the optical. There are sensors that detect pressure changes, steering patterns, weight distributions. Tools that gauge chemical signatures, energy levels, heart rates. You could disable the tracking of facial expressions and eye movements, eliminate head-pose estimation and gesture recognition and still be able to track and identify every passenger.

Even if you stick to basic verbal prompts you will disclose patterns of vocal inflection, variances of cadence and tone. Respiratory patterns can still be discerned even if you hardly say much of anything. It is not what you say that matters, people rarely express what they want to say anyway and we ourselves are usually too self-absorbed to notice. We rarely catch the undercurrents that disclose the truth—the energy coursing below the surface, circulating among bodies and spaces and bags. The electrophysiological vibrations bypassing the faculty of vision. There is much more data disclosed before a thought even becomes recognizable as an idea in the first place. Even before it enters the plane of speech, in the case of the AutoEgo—you do not need to say anything aloud when you are wearing the thing, it captures the signals the brain sends to the speech organs, converts the neuromuscular movements into words. Silent speech, they call it. Somewhere between thinking a thought and speaking it aloud. Your inner voice, brought one step closer to expression, but stopping just short of it.

It is the only way I could be recording these observations in detail without looking like a crazy person mumbling. Describing the scene even as I act in it. Modeling the world as a running story while living it, performing the moves. Just like the interior monologue people run in their heads all the time, but with the difference of having a record of it. Data to fill in the gaps, streamline disparities. Confirm decisions, contextualize actions.

I could hardly remember a thing otherwise, let me tell you. If human memory, as the Ego says, is becoming part of a longer history of technological advancement, then some level of outsourcing is going to be hard to avoid. The key is to be mindful of the limit, aware of that point where the advantages no longer outweigh the concessions. That point where the enhancements will no longer serve you, will become incompatible with what thinking should do. That is where you must draw a line.

The attendant seems to have finished his inquiry now, for he has turned toward his aggressors with a forbidding look, a look whose nature I know all too well, having been on the receiving end of it on many occasions.

They have a history—something on the record. Probably a drivescore lower than they realize, with no knowledge of how it was determined. No awareness of how much data has been collected or how it was acquired. Who is doing the analyzing, who is doing the categorizing, who is at the helm of the machine.

The two antagonists stare fixedly at the attendant, considering options. Now their arms swing into action. A reproachful gesture is made with a sharply pointed extremity, not an actual finger but a fingerlike tool, like a pincer, while another arm is swung emphatically toward the south end of the vestibule where another attendant is seated, peering out from behind a curbside counter.

It has become difficult to hear what anyone is saying as there is much honking and shouting going on. I can hear the Ego clearly of course, the signals go directly to the brain, you could stick your head out the window of a flying car and still hear and talk. Believe me, I know, I have done this.

One of the lanes has been cleared—the machine with the mechanical maw has started moving, freeing up the queue of vehicles waiting to exit. But there is a good deal of loudly expressed indignation directed at those who have been trying to nudge their way in.

One of these infiltrators—the right-to-weaponize sort, I can spot them immediately—has been blasting his horn, sticking his head out the window and howling.

A self-wheeling suitcase pulls up alongside him. Or a bot, I can never really tell the difference.

The attendant shakes his head firmly at the two aggressors, then lifts a hand to his head and stares open-mouthed, as if he cannot believe what he is seeing. He indicates, with a sweep of the hand, the inappropriateness of their bearing, then cranes his neck toward them to mirror it, adjust his stance to theirs. He stands with shoulders hiked up, back bent, arms akimbo and then, after generating sufficient parity to transmit the message, illustrates the state of their roadworthiness by widening his eyes, raising a forefinger to the area of his lower lid and sliding it downward, as if pulling on it.

It is very likely an alertness issue, a problem that requires tools for managing attention deficits. Gauging energy levels, diagnosing fatigue, monitoring cognitive load.

I must find out, I simply cannot go anywhere until I determine what the issue is with these two, learn the extent of the similarity we share.

The Ego provides no help as usual. Issues some abstract response. Hems and haws, tries to squeeze a complex idea into something vague. How the probability of this or that occurring grows or shrinks across this future, that future. Rather than just conveying the damn result.

The dauntless duo glare back at the attendant. They do not realize they are worsening their case, practically demonstrating their own need for stress management.

The monitoring systems are not just about tracking behavior, they are about influencing it. Not just about managing the behavior of the driver but making the driver more manageable.

The attendant raises a forefinger to his temple and taps it—a cognitive bandwidth problem, surely this must be it. He allows a few moments to pass and then positions his hands at both sides of his head in a manner suggestive of blinders. Some of the management systems are proactive, blocking out the exterior environment so as to eliminate potential triggers. They can also give you a little prod if needed, a stimulus to ensure you remain calm, keep your head up, eyes peeled.

Now he flicks his fingers in space, manipulating inputs. Then he moves his finger swiftly across the neck, indicating cut-off.

He is not one to be pushed around, this attendant.

I try to get a little closer to hear better, make a woe-is-me, melodramatic gesture of despair, as if the task of loading the trunk has been all too much for me, pressing the back of my hand to my forehead as I creep around the side of the car, my bottom sliding against the chassis as I drag the parcel that I have been trying to cram in the trunk with my free arm, my good arm, the one I use for show.

I realize the sight of someone so comparatively large performing this maneuver in a compression sheathcoat will likely invite attention, despite the coat's light-evading hue—stygian black, color of refusal, which absorbs nearly all radiation, turning any surface into what appears, to the sensors, to be a fathomless black hole.

A character in search of a plot.

Whether this analogy has come from my own self or not, I do not know—it is not always possible to establish the status of these thoughts until some time later, and even then, there is always the possibility of misattribution.

It could have been conveyed by the AutoEgo, encouraging me to put my deliberations into action, reminding me there are times when you must throw yourself into a scene, take the risk of bringing into play those interpersonal affinities that call you out of yourself, compel you to overcome the limits of your role. Affinities that arise out of nowhere, wrest you out of your comfort zone. Otherwise you just go on following the same old script, reproducing the same old lines.

I have always longed to be a part of something greater than myself. Especially those times when I feel I know a little too much about me. The Ego knows me most definitely, much more than it lets on. It knows, with an uncanny timing, precisely those moments when I need a little reminder, a little encouragement to take the chance, attune to the potentials of a situation, take the generative path forward rather than just spin my wheels, run around in circles.

I simply must find out what the issue is, find out whether the dauntless duo have had run-ins with the law, a high risk profile, anger management issues or something greater. There are programs that you cannot deactivate in those cases, like the one designed to prevent you from seizing the controls if you are prone to endangering yourself or others, experiencing a sudden urge to drive off a cliff, careen into oncoming traffic or something worse.

Another colleague of mine at the Institute is required to keep that program running wherever he goes. He says he can feel the system scrutinizing him silently, trying to size him up. As if it were thinking about how to get rid of him.

There are times when he will get in the car and just sit there, as if he were reluctant to give any input. The man cannot remember a thing, and there are times I do wonder if he has all but forgotten what you are supposed to do.

There are programs that insurance companies simply require, if you do not use them then your rates go up. The drunk driving one for instance.

I imagine that some contracts have a superego supplement, a proviso that on the surface seems reasonable, even benevolent, but which turns out to have a punishing aspect.

There are excesses that the system produces as a necessary outcome; they have to be eliminated in ways that cannot always be understood.

The program designed to prevent you from seizing the controls in a fit of road rage—you cannot turn that one off if you are prone to acts of retribution, have a history of tailgating, running people off the road or whatever. There have been quite a number of problems with that particular one. Believe me, I know. It has been known to identify an orgasm as road rage. And lock the driver out of the controls.

It is no surprise that some of these programs make people anxious, cause them to agonize over how the system is interpreting their emotional states. Some drivers go to great lengths to conceal any outward signs of distress. There are people I know who are skilled at modifying their appearance. Impression management—who doesn't do a bit of it? Engaging in the arts of indirection, indulging in a bit of duplicity to conceal signs of unease. Maneuvering subtly so as to maintain a veneer of nonchalance.

There are filters you can use to create a look of exuberance, induce an air of compassion, a demeanor of unrestrained joy. You can even opt to obscure features wholly, muddle the countenance so it cannot be made sense of at all.

The algorithms have learned to see through these countermeasures. They learn which signs are commensurate with a bearer's history, often the mere result of habit. Correlated to specific types of activity, personal preferences, environmental stimuli. Pattern-of-life data, the inferences drawn from it, the classifications based on it. This makes it easy to identify an expression that is ridiculously out of character, especially when it is obviously disproportionate to the context. The wide-eyed look of innocence, the selfless air of unbridled affirmation, the toothy grin of rapturous delight—these looks will, at a certain threshold, collapse beneath the weight of their own making. The driver will be locked out anyway.

2

City Center West

There was an accident at the construction site on the north side of the Crosstown. One of the excavation machines knocked a truck off the overpass. It created a huge bottleneck along the frontage road. We had to inch along in bumper to bumper traffic for nearly an hour.

People were patient at first, but then a few of the passengers started complaining in a way that caused everyone else to start complaining. A strange phenomenon happens in situations like that, suddenly everyone unloads, it releases a feeling of anguish but also excitement.

Everyone was speaking loudly in order to be heard above the noise. But it was hard to hear anything, you could only pick up bits and pieces of what people were saying. There was talk of accidents, anomalies, irrepressible crowds. A hearse chasing a group of tourists. A delivery truck menacing a passenger van. A parking lot brawl that got out of hand.

A traveler in the adjoining seat started talking to me. I found it hard to engage with him because he was wearing one of those facepieces that hide your expression. The only part that moves is a mouthlike orifice, a slot over the mouth for eating. Sometimes it snaps open and shut and you expect a voice to come out, but the voice does not come from there, it comes from an embedded speaker that has no relation to the mouth.

There is a much greater chance of misunderstanding if your face is hidden, I told him. It is better to have a transparent shield, like an astronaut. A bubble is better.

He started telling me about a mysterious car that was trailing him. A Compiler-type model that did nothing but follow him around. It would pull up to the house and sit there. Park outside the office and wait. He said he could feel it out there waiting for him even if he could not see it—one of those things you just know, like when you can feel someone staring at you without having to turn around to look.

I asked him if he had any idea of who might be in the car.

He had the sense that there was no one operating the car. That it was self-determined in some other way.

What way, I asked him.

Like the cars in those old road movies, he said. The ones that had no drivers but were self-operated somehow—powered by an unknown force. Limousines and hearses, towncars and trucks that appeared out of nowhere and chased people. Plowed into traffic, mowed down pedestrians, bumped off policemen, slammed into cars. Messengers of catastrophe, he called them. Self-aware, self-willed, superintelligent machines ready to strike, turn on the people they were created to serve.

A superintelligent machine would not act that way, I told him. It would be more like a conglomerate, more like a corporation than a vehicle. If you want to worry about a malevolent AI, that is what you should be concerned about. Not a machine that is out to get you, but an organization that is.

3

Beltway-Core Connector

The driver of the supercar enters the onramp with the brisk, cavalier urgency of a runway model. Checks his image on the display, switches to the ceiling-mounted camera and adjusts the tilt.

A moment of silent appraisal. The angle is not necessarily a flattering one, but the overall effect is radiant, golden light cast upon him through the aperture of the open sunroof, head perfectly aligned within the frame, accorded its rightful place at the center of the automotive cosmos.

He dabs his forehead to remove any sign of stress. The enormous pressure involved in achieving the right level of fluency on these drivestreams can under no circumstances be allowed to show. It has taken considerable effort to refine his style, which, as his admirers characterize it, combines the flair of a brand ambassador with the fervor of a conductor. A touch of the vaudevillian thrown in.

He is no mere narrator, this drivestreamer, he does not simply hawk product, does not merely describe automotive features but incorporates them into an exemplary state of existence, elevates them into a realm where he and his audience can join together, buoyed atop the inscrutability of the machine on which they sit, the chaos of the world through which they move and the fickleness of the authority that gauges their merit.

A moment of silent veneration. He is not a religious man, but he has learned to pay tribute to those divine forces that look after him—otherworldly powers whose workings we cannot know but which, provided we hold them in reverence, provided we remain humble before them, can show us that the very thing we regarded as a shortcoming might actually be a gift.

His tendency to blurt out uncontrollably for example, which has led him to resort to hand gestures alone in controlling the cameras, his head bucking and turbulent body sounds having been all too often mistaken for inputs, has now, as fate would have it, turned out to be an unexpected asset—one of the hallmarks of his appeal. One of the eccentricities that he had always tried to hide, tried his best to compensate for in order to avoid being ridiculed, but which he has since come to tolerate and even cultivate at times. He realized there must be something that others see in him that he is unable to see—a strange kind of appeal that he does not really understand and tries to avoid thinking about too much. The workings of human desire have always been opaque to him and if he does not need to deal with the subject then so much the better. If his gaffes and foibles are what boost his ratings then he might as well make the most of it, let the cameras roll, the roadshow roll on.

He has even learned to time his blunders for optimum effect. He has found, for example, that they become even more resonant against a backdrop of grandiloquence—prompting him to cultivate a little auto-aggrandizement here and there, learn to encourage those moments when his yearning to be taken seriously can be accented with a little vanity. In these moments it will be as if he himself were the agent of the car's magnificence, the features on which he expounds coincident with his own. The slip-ups that will often follow will arise naturally; they will be genuine, not necessarily authentic but sincere.

When he indulges in a bit of roguishness, the knowing wink that comes in the aftermath will have been in some sense honest, and when he takes the moral high ground, the indiscretion that inevitably pops up afterwards will have been involuntary, entirely unaffected and true: he could not help himself, had been seized by an unstoppable force, was forced to succumb.

Everyone is aware on some level they are acting, are they not? Performing for others what is supposed to be private.

In this manner he begins the present drivecast, letting loose with a belch so violent that the supercar itself seems to convulse, panning the ceiling-mounted unit in a round of sweeping motions along the interior of the vehicle as his hand, fingers jabbing, points out the features of the self-cleaning door panels, floorboards and bulkheads.

As the camera tracks along the bottom edges of the window frames, which together form a distinctly curved beltline that wraps around the entirety of the car, the hand makes a caressing move that seems vaguely obscene, all the more so as a crude comment is made about the shapeliness of the design, the reserve of ferocity beneath its sheath.

The feed from the dashboard unit is patched in as he bounces up and down in his seat to demonstrate the vibration compensator. The camera tilts downward to frame his midsection, which continues to jostle after he concludes the move.

Attention turns to the components of the supercar's situational enhancement system, a comprehensive end-to-end solution for amplifying awareness, supplementing driving functions as needed. A low-angle view is introduced from the center console unit, revealing a nominal control system with a nipple-like nub at the center.

The drivestreamer then rhapsodizes over the faculties of the simulation engine, extols its ability to provide actionable intelligence, amplify readiness, anticipate attack. He adds a suspenseful sound effect as he eulogizes its vulnerability assessment capacity, its ability to run adversarial models, emulate real-world threats.

The dashboard is slapped in a vigorous, swift motion, the rear-mounted camera kicks in and a spirited zoom-in to the console is implemented—revealing a projective simulation on the windowpane, shimmering in a delicate sapphire hue.

A shriek of delight goes up. He stares slack-jawed at the scene, imagines a Fire and Forget feature, a counteroffensive theme.

A moment of silent reflection. The drivestreamer knows he must check his enthusiasm on occasions like this; he does not want to appear overeager about a feature whose implications he has not sufficiently weighed. However confident he might be that the supercar's responsive, conciliatory veneer would diffuse any negative association, override any moral objection. Upon beholding it even the most belligerent footgoer would be compelled to back down, concede to its merits, submit to its charge.

A moment to relish the commanding feel, the vigorousness of heightened repute. His due, accorded him at last.

He lays his head back, mops his brow and cuts to the dashboard unit for a close-up.

The camera pans along the upper portion of the headrest, which extends upward in a semicircle, like a halo crown, then slowly zooms out to showcase the curvilinear, mindfulness-enhancing bolster that wraps around horizontally, covering the ears. The narrator glorifies the diagnostic features of the device, its ability to gauge attention levels, analyze vestibular-emotional reflex. Its potential to conduct emergency response notification is exemplified through an extension of the tongue, a clutching of the throat and the production of a gurgling sound.

The camera continues to zoom out as the features of the seatback as a whole are exhibited. Capacities extended, bodily bounds affirmed through the connecting, vibrating, sensor-rich sheath.

The drivestreamer squeals with delight as he catalogues the seat's ability to offer therapeutic rubdown, wiggling elatedly upon the ventilated, self-actuating surface as his own protuberant bottom is kneaded.

The seat's ability to conduct glandular manipulation sends him into a riotous spasm of guffawing, torso pitching, shoulders shaking, teeth flaring.

So overcome is he by these potentials that he does not notice the car's exit from the highway and the dilapidated Continental that is gaining on him from the rear. He rocks back and forth in waves of riotous chortling, head bobbing, skirt of hair jostling like the mane of a lurching horse.

Crosstown West

The analyst prefers to see clients in their own automobiles, scenography passing through the frame, the traffic rhythms, urban arrangements and streetscape panoramas forming a backdrop that helps to elicit recollection, set memory in motion. The road becomes a course, the course of a life, and every experience, as recounted, becomes a travel story that this type of therapy helps bring about. In her role as analyst she helps clients reevaluate their past, integrate subjective versions of their life experience with elements that emerge in the dialogical space of the psychoanalytic interaction.

The process works best when her clients are riding in the vehicle of their choice. But the vehicle preferred by this particular client—one of the Aerocars that her company, Metro Traffic, makes available to reporters of her caliber—feels overly sequestered and hermetic, like a spaceship. It provides no opportunity for memories to be integrated with the scenery they pass along the way: the projected models that flicker across the windowpanes depict the landscape as a horizon of ever-renewing abstraction, a resplendent, elaborately signaled world that is only made visible through calculation.

The analyst knows that, as far as this client is concerned, the alternatives are even worse. They lack the potential for on-the-spot traffic reporting that a vehicle like this one affords—the immediate response capability that will allow her client to relax, take time out to talk freely. The anxiety of insufficient availability can be difficult for a reporter like her to manage without the right trade-offs, especially at this particular moment in her life, when she has found herself in the midst of a crisis, approaching that critical stage where something fundamental has changed and she finds it hard to go on as before. A situation made all the worse for its resistance to being claimed as a problem, summoned and conveyed in words.

The sublime world of traffic that she once knew intimately now appears flat and unperturbed, devoid of the tension that is an essential part of its nature. Once rife with imperative, it now flows like a tranquil stream, empty of friction and feature. The very thing that once revved her up, sharpened her senses, honed her skills for the challenges to come has moved on without her, leaving her parked in her car, staring at the screen like some bored functionary while all around her the world surges on, realigns and hastens toward arrangements that she can no longer see, domains she cannot access, operations she can no longer run.

That momentum that had always sustained her, that motivating force that always carried her, motored her onward, kept her going, had always been implicit, innate to whatever she did, now seems to lack some crucial aspect, some core component that needs to be replenished. And she finds herself longing for some exotic factor that could energize it: an act that destabilizes, a catastrophe that unifies, enlivens, unleashes recreative force.

The reporter had begun speaking of the amusement park she used to visit as a child. Recalling her fondness for those little mock sportscars with thick rubber bumpers that allow you to slam into other vehicles with force. Recalling how the collisions would resound, echo off the metal surfaces of the arena, mix with the thrumming of drivetrain and the surging of wind. She would become so immersed in the dynamic of the ride in those moments that her thoughts would cease and the distinctions between body and machine fade away. Her sense of self would be revitalized, as if it were supplementary to the act.

She has now turned her attention to the images that have arrayed themselves on the frontward panels of the Aerocar. Models of traffic that materialize, register patterns of the moving, participate in the mobilization of the measured. Facets that loom thickly in the air, but which are only made visible through the projections that can illumine them, like the night fog that appears only under headlight. Registers of intelligibility that pass through one another, otherwise unseen. Coursing along like roads, overlaying and unfolding like dreams.

She stares fixedly at a spot along the Crosstown, her thoughts turning toward an incident that has appeared, a sequence of events condensed into images and about to be transformed, elevated into narrative.

Like a clairvoyant, the reporter probes these illusive foreshadowings; like a philosopher, she deciphers implications in the codes that stream by. She can intuit the hidden dimensions of the accident, the underflow that transforms action into event. The spectacle that holds drivers in its sway like a procession of the devout, offers sanctification along the contours of the collision, the reassurance that one can gain intimacy with death and move on.

She is not the kind of reporter who settles for rote determinations. She does not pave over uncertainties, reduce anomalies to the known, resolve them to descriptions alone. She knows she must provide insights that are not reproducible if she wants to stay relevant. She knows she must push at the limits of speech, tap undercurrents that programs cannot reach. Otherwise traffic becomes featureless, recedes as an object. And she along with it.

There is no competing with the algorithms, the AI systems that help contour the traffic they analyze, building a continuously updated model with all places interpretable, all things machine-readable, layered over the physical environment in accordance with real-time equivalents and synchronized, roused into coherence in form. Not simply a model of traffic for drivers to query but a system that performs its own meaning, constitutes its own controlling, provides its own best explanation.

Defining movement in the act of mapping it. Constituting traffic in the act of representing it.

What makes a reporter stay relevant is her ability to uncover something other, something alien yet foundational, incalculable yet sustaining. Her ability to channel the unfathomable in the events she covers, unearth a senseless undercurrent, that which escapes meaning, composition, words.

Hands raised to eye level, fingers outstretched and flexing, the reporter modulates the arrangements on the displays. Gestures conveying sense. Scaling to the right level to receive. Attuning to the right register to know, become inherent to the flow.

Lot in Life

The driver of the Conquest pulled into the northmost entrance of the parking lot, preparing for drop-off. He sat buoyantly in his seat, thankful that vehicles have come to function as valets, relieving us of the burdensome task, once unavoidable, of prowling the lots in search of a vacant stall. It was all the more troubling, then, that the Conquest overshot the mark, sped past the drop-off zone like a plane hurtling down the runway—a malfunction that immediately brought to mind the problem he experienced earlier, an error that he took to be minor at the time but which, he now realized, was part of a much more critical issue that should have been addressed. The wellness program had detected his elevated heart rate correctly, but rather than initiating the palliation sequence to ease the rising stress levels, it activated the energizing routine.

A surge of anxiety now overtook him as the Conquest hurtled forth into the depths of the lot. It zigzagged through the concrete labyrinth of aisles, approached an open space, and prepared for entry.

A much more serious malfunction now became apparent: the door would not unlock. If he could not manage to disembark before the car entered the stall he would be hopelessly penned in, side clearances in these lots having been reduced to little more than a hand's breadth.

He swung toward the latch on the passenger door—likewise disabled.

He jabbed his fingers in the air, swept his palms side to side, and thrust his elbows downward and up as if by means of these gestures a command might be issued.

Pitching downward, arms outstretched, he ran his fingers along the dashboard in search of a manual override. To no avail.

As the car began to enter the space, he raised his head above the console like a soldier peering out of a trench, gripped with a sense of impending doom.

A cluster of whirring sounds ensued, followed by a tiny blip.

Then, silence.

He lunged at the driver's side door, pawed at the inscrutable surfaces of the door panels, rummaged through the recesses of the console bin.

Then he reached into the side pocket to retrieve his phone.

The agent who answered his call was friendly and sympathetic. She attempted to unlock the doors remotely, then made several bids to restart the engine. He remained upright and stock-still as she worked, eyes darting side to side, eagerly awaiting the familiar sound of a click. He heard only the whisper of the highways in the distance.

The agent sensed his rising agitation, advised him to be patient and introduced a calming sequence of ambient notes. She is trained to assess physiological states, correlated with historical values and emotion metrics to deliver contextually relevant solutions, while establishing an emotional connection between the company and each individual driver.

Try not to do anything rash, she said.

With a glimmer of paranoia he wondered what it was, exactly, she ventured he might do. And how the possibility could have been formulated. He knows that whatever sense of parity he might feel with these agents is an illusion. Their ability to assess your fears and aspirations so astutely, before you are even aware of having had them yourself—how vast was the well from which it drew?

Gusts of wind swept about the lot, circulating heat among the densely packed agglomeration of machines. The dispatching of a service truck had done little to assuage his anxiety, for he now thought only of what could befall him while he waited in despair, a wretched and pitiable figure condemned to an untimely fate.

He clutched at his chest, rolled back and forth on the therapeutic seat, gasped for breath, wheezed.

He wiped the sweat off his forehead with the back of his hand.

You fool, he mumbled. Here you are. Stripped of standing, dispossessed of footing. The traction for escape, the stability for defending.

The agent was back on the line. Sit tight, she said. Help is on the way.

A terrible thought seized him: His boss will be furious! He will be late, very late! The prospect of committing yet another blunder gripped him with dread. He would be ridiculed again. Cut down to size.

He peered through the steam-coated window, palms to the glass.

Help!

His muffled calls went unnoticed by the few souls that milled about, inhabitants being scant in this immense metropolis of machines. Dense, rigorously aligned amalgamations that required little differentiation until the need occasioned it, like so many of the automotive groupings into which drivers entered. Aggregates seen from the street, the operations center, the control hub. Merged across the cabins and movement flows, to be set apart only as the need for scrutiny arose. Some aggravating factor disrupting. Some malevolent actor approaching. Some obstruction to eliminate, some culprit to capture. The location of an incident heralded by an emergency alert.

Help!

Until then, asymmetries are absorbed into the background domain, no input required. Onlookers oblivious to your plight. There is not much difference between the passenger and the vehicle at these scales. Corporeality extends and retracts, wells up and dilutes. Intentions are deciphered through the actions of the car.

It is generally the case that he is overlooked, he reminded himself. Invisible in the scheme of things.

The agent was back. Sit tight, she said. Help is on the way.

They might not notice me, he replied. They seldom do.

Even the most obvious thing can hover like a ghost, she said. Invisible to those present and near. The actuality can fade into a silhouette while the illusion hardens into a fact. The alert responded to is not always apparent to those standing there. The obstacle detected a majority of drivers will not see.

They will not see me, he said.

Machines of the most profound effect can be invisible to those they serve, she said. Always on, always running. Placeless, timeless, endless and as nothing.

Help, he said.

And she said, Help is here.

4

Fusion Center

I jumped into the back seat of the car I had summoned, only to have the agent address me by a different name. Evidently the vehicle, a Compiler, had been ordered by someone else, but that person was heading to the same place I was, and before I had time to think about it, I found myself going along—sliding into the role as easily as I slid into the car. It seemed the appropriate thing to do, as if I had selected this option when I made the booking. As elementary as switching parts, as effortless as merging into a different lane. Partaking of the continuance it affords. Acquiescing to its conditions, its cooperative demands. Bathing in the flows of its norm.

Central Avenue Plaza

A procession of cars is heading toward the Institute for Automotive Intelligence at the end of the avenue. A location once framed by strip malls and superstores, open-air markets and grand promenades, now overshadowed by a boundless superhighway, a thoroughfare that leads nowhere, a thruway in which places disappear.

The occupants of this automotive procession will not be hailed by the revamped shopping mall they presently approach, will not enter its restyled passageways, will not traverse its emporia—they are headed toward the cavernous underground garage, a vast subterranean netherworld that the Institute had little use for until it was transformed into a drive-in meeting center, even though its structure is far from ideal for assemblies of this type.

The sloped floors cannot be altered, but they no longer induce the kind of anxiety they once did among the ambulating shoppers from the retail center that loomed above, shoppers who, dismayed by the inconvenient stairwells, often resorted to ambling along the perilously steep ramps in search of their automobiles, which due to the obscure organizational scheme, were always difficult to find. Navigation between floors, no less venturing out on foot, is no longer needed since each of the two levels on which meetings are held operates independently of the other. The median strip on each floor provides a central hub around which attendants convene.

The ability to hold in-person meetings without need of disembarkation has given new life to structures like this, allowing attendees to exchange their own protective gear for the automobile's intrinsic safeguarding provision. It allows the industry consortium leaders who have convened this particular meeting—affiliates in automotive and infrastructure intelligence, transportation analytics, manufacturing, mobility services, contracting, lobbying, and the like—to maintain the relative anonymity they require. They need to keep a low profile at this stage in order to avoid the kind of misunderstanding that could adversely affect their public relations, stir up discontent among the audience they need to persuade. The initiatives they are promoting, which aim to transform key sections of the highway infrastructure into autonomous driving corridors known as Autocades, are highly unpopular with those who drive manually, a significant portion of the populace. The consortium leaders have no wish to exacerbate the misconceptions that attend these initiatives, many of which have already taken hold negatively in the public mind. The need to counter these mistaken impressions is the reason the founders of the consortium have gathered. They aim to soften the opposition by developing a uniform media strategy, clear up the confusion with a public service campaign.

The exclusionary nature of the Autocades does not make the task any easier. The level of synchronization necessary for the highways to function leaves no possibility of compromise. Every vehicle must be suitably equipped, choreographic cohesion cannot happen without across-the-board algorithmic control, it only takes one manually-operated vehicle to destabilize the whole.

The members of this consortium are well aware of the need to adopt a congenial tone in their communications, approach these matters with sensitivity and tact. They understand that the automobile has always been coincident with the notion of autonomy, embodying ideals of individuality and self-determination in its very frame. The symphony of aptitudes provided by the vehicle is one that drivers have always been able to share, the repertoire of capabilities they draw on reducible, at least in theory, to a singular form roughly equivalent to their own. The consortium leaders know they must strike a sympathetic note, identify with the nature of the resistance if they are to ease public anxiety and foster a sense of optimism, inspire a renewed sense of confidence in the forms of intelligence that are emerging in the urban world, forms that are already present in everyday life, ingrained in conveyances people already use, the actions of systems they are already a part of, but are unable to see. They regard the developments of intelligent transport as wholly liberating—empowering individuals to lead better lives, boosting desirable social qualities and enriching community bonds. Some of them can even see in the algorithmic coordination an emergent form of empathy, the kind of fellow-feeling that comes into play though interactional alignments, the choreographic synchronicity of common rituals, the iterative assurance of customs shared among communities, recurrent programs and routines. Practices that have always been enabled by machines.

The consortium representatives have been aided in this effort by their colleagues at the Institute's Explainability division—researchers who are helping to develop accessible terminology, find metaphors for conveying a sense of how intelligent systems work in ways that non-experts can understand. The fact that driving has played such a foundational role in the modern era makes the work less onerous: there are few practices as widely shared as driving; the principles and techniques, instruments and imaginaries of automotive life are ingrained at the level of the body and the urban population as a whole, from the culture of the community to the larger symbolic horizon from which the whole experience of transit is drawn. The very means of conveyance, the capacity to move from place to place. The platforms and affinities of automotive life involve people and machines together in a shared system, a shared order of intelligibility that has been operative since the advent of motoring, and remains operative even now.

There are always going to be problems, of course, with systems of this scale and complexity. The incidents that have recently happened are an obvious concern; the consortium has no wish to overlook them. At the same time the organization strives to keep an eye on the bigger picture, situate the anomalies within a more constructive long-term view. The manually-operating throng has been quick to seize upon these incidents and blow them out of proportion, blame them on software and systemic failing even as the consortium's automotive and transport industry constituency has thoroughly revealed them, time and time again, to be the result of human error—the majority of them due to these very same drivers fumbling with controls that they are ill-equipped to handle, controls that should be snatched from them entirely and integrated into the car itself.

Needless to say, these holdouts are not looked upon kindly. While the consortium takes great care to project an image of benevolence in its public-facing communications, the sentiment behind closed doors could hardly be less charitable to the organic operators with whom the machine is required to share the road, the fleshy counterparts with which the algorithms must reason if an efficient transport choreography is to be achieved. The fact that the autodriven vehicle's primary objective is to avoid the heedless moves that these drivers tend to make—lurching into crosswalks, careening across lanes, cutting off pedestrians, barreling through intersections—makes the resistance all the more unbearable, especially when it results in accidents that could easily have been prevented.

The task of accommodating this mortal element is one that the logic of systems optimization has been primed to reject. The body remains extricable from the machine, cognition from matter. If driving is to be posed as a problem, rendered addressable in ways that software can solve, then there is only one logical solution, only one possible course of action: it is the paradoxical, wild-eyed human at the helm that is to be shown the door, the indolent body perched at the wheel, fearful and prone to distraction, easily riled by absurd, capricious needs, plagued by quizzical resentments and mindless delusions.

The only sensible way forward is algorithmic: logical operations unswayed by the vagaries of corporeal life.

A focus on safety issues has been deemed to have the best chance of success for the campaign, based on the assumption that when push comes to shove, the reduction of injury and death is the concern that outweighs all others in the public mind. No one can dispute the priority of saving lives, especially when supported by data that appears irrefutable, statistics that seem inviolably clear. The ability of the algorithmic system to react to environmental variance is far superior to the response time of even the most attentive human; data pertaining to speed, position, direction, and road conditions is shared, interpreted, cross-analyzed, and converted into action in timeframes so infinitesimally small they can hardly be described, no less understood.

The advantage of massively distributed computation and control is so conclusive as to be absolute.

Indeed it is so comprehensive as to be divine, as the senior media influencer in the Emancipator XL towncar puts it, searching for the right tagline. It absolves the people—saves them from themselves!

Saviors of the people! proclaims an equipment manufacturer, waving a handlike implement out the window of the Aporia Premier.

Saviors! the executive in the neighboring car honks.

Saviors! is repeated in the air. The reverberation generated by the immense concrete surfaces of the underground hollow—which can at times introduce confusion as to who is actually speaking or being addressed—is conducive to utterances of a more direct nature, expressions devoid of unnecessary baggage and conveyed bluntly, condensed into an imperative of some sort.

The crisis of highway mortality—solved! exclaims the CEO of a security firm, striking the dashboard with a fist.

Solved! reverberates in the air.

The Nemesis Premium honks.

We should not rely on logic, says the meeting head, who has parked in the reserved spot at the north end of the central median strip in a GDH sedan whose stealthy veneer—which decreases contrast between the bodyframe and its surrounding to minimize visual footprint—permits no glimpse of the speaker through the window. The effect is suggestive of an offscreen presence, the kind of atmospheric authority conveyed by one of those cinematic figures obscured in a chiaroscuro of shadows, figures whose position outside the realm of visibility seems to heighten their influence, channel their power into the vocal and increase it by virtue of the displacement.

Does not our sensorium vibrate with the very threat that our thoughts would compel us to deny? says the voice. That dangerous and irresolute outside that in our fascination we draw near.

The fact that the meeting head is parked on the downslope seems to escalate the unsteadying consequences of the floor gradient, which, although only minimal in the primary meeting area along the central median between the two double-loaded parking bays, increases substantially in the vicinity of the drive aisles. It provokes an inherent sense of possessiveness, as if at any moment the proceeding might go downhill, the movables involved in the undertaking roll downward along the declivity. Lending the sense that ground must be held, positions clung to, wheels and heels dug in.

The vague outline of the GDH sedan flickers as the voiceover continues.

Does not safety draw its resonance from the hazard that looms, the danger against which one could brush and whose variable force one might activate in a resurgent form? The unknowable encounter, from whose energetic undercurrent one could draw. That imperiling force, dangerous and irrational, at the basis of the transit world.

A chorus of honking erupts, signaling assent.

Let us work the knife-edge ratio between fear and reward. One that could be fine-tuned with each installment.

Three honks from the far end, echoing across the median.

Close your eyes and imagine that exceptional moment when you, the everyday streetgoer, stride blithely into the road. Trusting that even the most maniacal driver will stop in time, only to be caught in that perilous instant when you realize they might not.

Two horn beeps, echoing.

Imagine that moment when you, the ordinary viewer, have to avert your eyes from the impending calamity, only to be drawn back into its galvanizing center, its bonding swell of lurid fascination.

One beep.

That horrifying scene from which you cannot flee. That roadside spectacle you cannot look at but must see.

Beep.

In the uproar: an unmistakable desire for more.

More, is repeated.

At that point might we harness the power to convince, stoke the kind of arousal that sediments into belief.

Belief.

The kind that, once it gains momentum, sources what it needs for its powering and orients actions in accordance with its parameters and rules, however logical or illogical the tenets, as it gathers force, stabilizes into a platform, consolidates into a moving train that you now must sustain.

5

Science Park

The researchers in the Explainability division know that intelligent machines are unlikely to become trusted collaborators if no one can understand their inner processes—the operations behind the conclusions they arrive at, the rationales behind the decisions they make. The experts are not much help in this area. They have a hard time clarifying the inner workings even to themselves, you can hardly expect them to explain them to others. Were they to attempt an explanation, it would hardly be comprehensible or relevant to people outside their field. It would probably not even be interesting enough to try to get through in the first place. The language would be too opaque, the sphere of applicability too limited. It would suffer from a lack of detail, or be overburdened by it.

Some of us have questioned whether a straightforward technical-scientific interpretation is really the best way to go about it. There is a speculative leap required no matter what you do. An element of fictionalizing.

Our team has been experimenting with a narrative approach. Using narratives to perform the function of explanation. We have been training algorithms to create them rather than depending on human intermediaries.

It is not as strange as it might seem. People use narratives to explain how they arrive at the decisions they make all the time, even if they do not know what is really going on in their minds and often get it wrong.

The process is worthwhile even if it does not generate usable results. It helps the AI systems to improve, add to their communication skills, learn new rhetorical strategies. Gain insight into kinds of narratives that work, connect with the impulses according to which they are formed. Learn how to script realistic and relatable scenes. Influence the kinds of attitudes that stories are influential in shaping.

It may well be the case that a narrative model will be able to circumvent some of the barriers that inhibit the impact of straightforward interpretation. It might help overcome the kinds of presumptions that get in the way. If it is the form that people prefer, the form they commonly use to make sense of one another, understand events, interpret motives, comprehend actions, then perhaps it is the best choice for the job. If it works for people, who are harder to make sense of than machines, then it should work for machines.

6

Mid-City Interchange

Among the most visible opponents of the new highway is a parish, an ecclesiastical acropolis that once enjoyed the privileges of extraterritoriality, but which is now on the verge of being supplanted, overthrown by a roiling infrastructure whose disruptions it once helped quell.

Already suffering indignities on a daily basis on account of the roaring concrete thruways that veer perilously close, disrupt invocations, mute the pealing of bells, the elders who govern the district have pursued every means available to ward off the looming incursion, compel state authorities to rescind their approval of the highway on the basis of the constitutional protections it will violate, the burdens it will impose, the restrictions it will place upon the devout.

The right to worship must be defended at all costs, the freedoms of the practicing upheld above all other measures: the massive concrete firmament, if constructed, will impede the transcendental order, derail devotional connection, upstage ceremonial progression, block access to the divine. The spire atop the cathedral tower, designed to focalize the spirit, elevate the look, vilipend the earthly in favor of the highest heavenly exaltation, will be consigned to the underside of a ramp.

As a gesture of respect for the elders, the acting Deputy Administrator for the Transportation Commission arranged for a special hearing—securing for this purpose the Grand Officiator, a model equipped with enhanced passenger awareness and acoustic control, which not only filters out unwanted noise but differentiates among the individual vocal output of each passenger and muffles, supplements, or replaces undesired conversation in each particular area. Enhancing interior scene transcription through learned experience.

Analytical surveys were presented by the state counsel, addressed to the three ecclesiastics seated in the back and the adjudicator who sat next to her in front. They were intended to demonstrate that the motoring public, if given the choice, would prefer to partake of devotional services in the car rather than the chapel itself. Surveys among the broader churchgoing public revealed that 38% could not leave their cars without feelings of impending doom, which as regards attendance at religious services placed them in the unjust predicament of having to calibrate torments to be endured one way or the other. Among the congregants themselves, 63% actually felt closer to the Almighty while driving; for manual drivers, gunning the engine could produce a surge of divine energy, while for those with a proclivity for the autodrive, relinquishing the controls generated a stimulating, if not paradoxical, dynamic, allowing transubstantiation of the body without disrupting the assurances of the seat in which the bottom could remain firmly lodged—secured within the arms of an enclosure that protected against threats of loss just as it did from the ravages of speed and environmental inclemency.

One must see the driver as a swivel, the counselor declared: operational movements of the hand, foot, and head may be stilled, yet the body is roused and exerted on new fronts, corridors of action aligned with the motivity of the vehicle. The car becomes the means of instilling a new sense of movement in the world, one that is exceedingly active, unhindered and unconfined.

By means of these assertions the counselor attempted to position the state on the side of the public, affirming the rights of the faithful to choose and defending them against those who would deny them these rights, impose on them the unjust dictate of having to motor to the chapel and disembark from the car.

Expropriation of the parish grounds would place no limitation on the freedom to worship. It would amplify that freedom.

Aware that such an argument would have little chance of success without precedents, the counselor supported it with the presentation of religious institutions who had already begun to offer services en route, and therefore, who now acted in the public good. Churches that were addressing the growing legions of drivers for whom the demands of automotive operation no longer called, and who now had a good deal of extra time on their hands, which the Almighty tends to discourage.

In highlighting these features, the counselor cleverly steered them away from the context of the luxury option and instead situated them among the fail-safe mechanisms as a whole: devices that provided a buffer against error, interpreted decisions before they were carried out in order to compensate for detected neglect.

Her first example was the so-called Guardian Angel system, geared to take the wheel when the algorithms detected the driver going astray, careening out of control, or committing a regrettable error. This example was followed by the demonstration of a more comprehensive package, still in development, which supplements the Angel system with an added roster of driver assists for crises of an ethical and ontological nature—making subtle adjustments and absolutions for moral predicaments and seizing complete control if a greater catastrophe looms, although, just like the Angel system, only to the extent it is needed, after which it vanished, much like an antilock brake.

She did not mention that tests of these systems have been found to be problematic if not life-threatening by traumatized motorists battling with their divine overseer in the throes of transit, often due to the perception that it was placing imagined obstructions in their paths, issuing indecipherable commands, inveighing against those who lacked the feature, or triggering ominous warning lights that would not go off.

The three ecclesiastics, having largely restrained their indignation, could take no more. They expressed their opposition to what they understood as a blasphemous equivalence between the Almighty and the antilock brake.

The junior clergyman grasped his iron cross, inviolate device, and held it aloft, inadvertently dislodging a ceiling dome light with its extremity as the trio swayed side to side.

The counselor craned her head toward them politely, indicating she meant no disrespect. She clarified that the antilock brake she referred to was not, in effect, an entity but a sequence of commands, imparting motion through means that hardly had anything to do with the lowly foot. It too was unswayed by the vicissitudes of corporeal life and in this, conveyed an authority that could not be denied. In that it issued from a known rather than an unknowable source it actually improved upon the matter, instantiating a symbolic order that was no longer abstract, no longer plagued by needless mystification and wrongful interpretation, without any diminishment of its larger informing amplitude.

Sensing the clergymen's alarm at this prospect, she told them to fear not, for much of it remained unfathomable:

I am speaking of an informing surround that is larger than ourselves, but which is comprised of techniques and procedures that can be accounted for and refined; a sphere of sensory intelligibility that driverbelievers can draw on and by way of its operationalization define.

The ecclesiastics listened with bowed heads, fidgeting.

Even though much remains unfamiliar at the scale and speed of each individual driverbeliever, she added, they can operate in accordance with the terms of the ethereal address, whole in their confidence, secure in their position and bearing.

The group lurched to the right as the Grand Officiator took an abrupt turn.

The counselor threw her head back, gazed skyward, and raised her arms:

O elastic intimacies! Long had you been heralded by automotive travel, but constrained due to the operational requirements involved. Can you not now be freely indulged?

The adjudicator eyed her uneasily.

O driving bodies! Can you not join the ranks of the unfettered redundancies, freed from your mounts like the steering wheel and brake pedal, speed bump and signboard?

The three ecclesiastics fell upon one another as the car banked northward and veered around the edge of a reservoir. They consulted for a brief interval and then arranged themselves to deliver, in the style of a recitative, their response:

Able court! We who have heard the sound of surveys intoning, of devices ringing, extolling virtues. We, messengers of the Spirit. We, servants of the Lord, vessels of the Word, vehicles of the Will. Let it be known, what studies have shown. Drivers, driving around in circles. Advancing, looping, retreating. Driving, circling, searching.

For a parking spot? the counselor asked.

The elder cleric leaned forward, grabbed the edges of the passenger seat and pulled himself up behind her.

They were referring to the interminable quest—the wheel of deferral. The delusion of finally having arrived, followed by the demand to depart once more.

The triad fell silent for a moment, then added:

The opening that is sought—does not exist.

The counselor voiced her disagreement, offering to demonstrate the parking assistance feature as proof.

7

Downtown Hub

The Human Impulse Study focuses on individuals who are inclined toward aggressive behavior. People who try to thwart the autodriven vehicle in some way, whether through subtle acts of intimidation or outright attempts to obstruct its competency, cloud its perception, throw it off course. Maneuvering erratically in order to taunt. Moving impulsively in order to befuddle. Swerving fitfully, careening maniacally. Riding roughshod.

Not only drivers—footgoers, too. Bystanders who harass the intelligent vehicle for no apparent reason. Lurching unexpectedly into crossings to make the cars stop. Gesturing incalculably, trodding inscrutably. Muscling in. They know that for each vehicle compelled to screech to a halt for an unpredictable human that has ambled into its path, the effects will ripple. Scores of overreactive machines will soon beguile the streets.

It has always been expected that the rationales for this kind of behavior would elude understanding, vary as greatly as the implicit *rules of the road* that are often cited, so wildly inconsistent they could hardly be called rules at all. But the inner impulses, the predispositions ingrained so deeply that the subjects themselves cannot access them—these are thought detectable with the right methods. The Impulse Study presumes that an accurate estimation of these tendencies will enable the system to make better inferences, improve its ability to anticipate what people are likely to do and from that basis, prepare the appropriate response. Thereby allowing the vehicle's response time to be improved, its sensitivity level fine-tuned.

Some of the scientists at the Institute have the wrong idea about the work we are doing. A good deal of the misunderstanding comes from the division heads, who are convinced we are presupposing an individual psyche—a psychogenic base in which the root of human motive resides. We do not operate on any such premise and we take every opportunity to disabuse them of this notion. We regard the human body the same way they do—an aggregate of neural and biochemical subsystems with no psychic apparatus presumed to be in there calling the shots. Yet the misunderstanding persists. They cannot seem to let go of the idea. It is like they are obsessed with it.

My perspective is pretty limited, admittedly. But I think I have an idea of what the problem is. I think the problem for the skeptics is not the approach itself but the scale at which it is applied. In their mind the analysis is best accomplished at a level much broader than that of the individual—a level that stretches from minute bodily subsystems to the collective domains of societal and historical life, scales up to bypass the self as the mediator between internal and external existence. If expressive tendencies are to be examined they see no point in looking anywhere other than to these larger systems, which are so pervasive and wide-ranging that they have come to play a formative role in shaping the reality they measure. They generate predispositions more than merely register them, provide orientations and inclinations for the automotoring life.

There is some truth to this. These are the very domains that people themselves look to for answers pertaining to their own impulses, their own impending choices, their own desires and motives. The inherent principles that guide the course of their being. The stimulus and the steering. But the skeptics take it too far. They maintain that there is no need to know anything at all about people to anticipate what they do, hardly any need to look under the hood, hardly any need to inquire into the source of action, ask the question of what drives, how motive comes about, whether turns are taken deterministically, directions chosen randomly or freely.

It is not as if they themselves have the answers, though, and most of them are wise enough to keep quiet about it, at least within earshot of the Institute higher-ups. They are well aware of their own shortcomings and they know that our team, if provoked, is not averse to calling attention to this lack.

On the chance that our approach might turn out to prove workable it does not make much difference anyway, the matter of how impulses are actually determined need not be resolved. If it helps eliminate precious microseconds of response time, helps make the connection between the system's behavior and its code more immediate, it does not matter how it was accomplished. We do not need to know how internal determinations are made—we only need to know how competent the applications are. Just as we do not need to know the mechanisms of our own understanding in order to be able to react appropriately, optimize our ability to respond and learn.

Since my job as a technician is fairly low-level, I circulate more than the scientists do and pick up comments that would not be voiced if the higher-ups were around. No one pays much attention to me and I overhear things that people say when no one important is there. I know, for example, that the division heads have been trying to pull our funding, and from what I can gather, it is largely because of them that the in-field resources the motorist team relies on have dwindled. Not only our team but the pedestrian team too. I do not think it is solely because of the psychic aspect I mentioned. I think it is a symptom of some larger problem they have, some overriding perception of us that they simply cannot bear. But I cannot figure out what it is. It really does seem beyond reason.

We have to be all the more circumspect, choose our words carefully, use the right descriptors. When we talk to those who have a tendency to misinterpret our research we use terms that are less likely to be construed as psychological. We opt for terms like motoring energy instead of inner impulse, for example. We try to stay at the level of attributes and operations without mentioning the substrates. Like describing a powertrain without the car, traffic without the road, waves without reference to the sea.

The devices worn by our test subjects lend themselves well to this approach. They are so integrally connected to the vehicle that they might as well be part of it. The physiological monitoring conducted by the sensor strap, which extends upward from the floorboard and wraps across the midsection, is an easy extrapolation of what the car already does, integrating bodily functions as part of its key performance indicators—markers of speed and position, stop and start intervals, engine revolution, power consumption and so on.

So too with the sentiment profiles, dispositions inferred from physiological responses, bodily expressions and behavioral patterns. Routine elements of lifecycle management systems.

The cognitive monitoring performed by means of the transcranial cap is a notable exception. Its purpose is to detect those elusive neural events that register a decision to act before the driver is aware of having made the choice, and in this, reveal the hidden dimension of impulse determination that has long evaded observation-based techniques. The device is somewhat familiar from experiments in mind-controlled operation, studies where an electromagnetic field is directed toward specific brain areas to measure and manipulate electrical patterns for cognitive enhancement—a human effectiveness training that augments awareness, locates it within a shared field of deliberation and action that becomes immanent to the system, bounded in no particular body or car. Our device is not outfitted for that purpose.

We try to disregard the cap's unflattering aesthetic, the veneer of cranial depilation it imposes and the way it tends to make the face look distended. Admittedly, the effect has the potential to trigger sensory and behavioral responses in other people who might encounter it suddenly, which might have an influence on the phenomena it helps analyze. But the appearance of the driver is not understood to be a factor in the study, it is only the overall impression the car makes that is understood to be significant. The vehicle's own entry onto the scene is acknowledged as a factor that must be taken into account in the probabilistic models, but the appearance of the driver is bundled into it, the relevant contingencies displaced to the cabin exterior, cap consolidated into car. The subjects could undergo some radical metamorphic shift and it would not matter. No attention is paid to the effects of the encircling strap, which runs continuously down the jawline and cups the chin, making the exposed front appear aggressively thrust forward while the massive lower sheath exerts upward pressure on the jowls. Giving rise to a grimace that can appear maniacal or malicious at times, especially when seen from the front.

A blind eye is also turned to the compression of the forehead executed by the weighty central panel at the top, which adds a glowering aspect.

The cumulative impression is one of adrenalized and restrained anguish, it must be said. As if the test subject were consumed by some burning need but constrained from achieving it, pushing against the limits that have been imposed and about to burst through, impelled to act but unable to move.

At times it is the look of someone who has suddenly jolted themselves upright from a traumatic nightmare and found themselves thoroughly agitated, unable to process the environment into which they have now awakened, unable to interpret the scene, update the model, translate sensory data into commands. While being forced that very moment to act.

It is quite understandable, then, why the sudden glimpse of a test subject on the highway could be so alarming for those who have not been exposed to the phenomenon previously. Causing some drivers to overreact.

You do have to wonder whether the test subjects might court this power themselves to some extent. Assume over time the qualities that the gear elicits. Its dispositional leaning, its symbolic calling.

How often has it been that I myself, among the least who would be thought susceptible to such influences, have entered into just this sort of circumstance and succumbed. My own face in the mirror, illuminated by the intermittent burst of passing headlamps, barely recognizable to me in the cabin's dim light. The expressions I unintentionally make while driving, so often misinterpreted by others, are in these instances heightened in their emotional connotations—not necessarily with the Compiler I have recently been taking, which is rather ordinary, but in a very pronounced way with the dilapidated Continental I sometimes drive and cannot seem to part with despite its many disfigurements, especially its crushed front grille and mangled, baroquely protrudent bumper, which causes those I encounter to be stricken with unease at the sight, as if I and the vehicle had harnessed the accident's power, had become the agent of the destructive force it embodied. Prompting them to keep their distance or otherwise quickly get out of the way.

So I can imagine how some drivers could find this power rewarding or stimulating in some way. Cultivate it unconsciously, assimilate it inadvertently over time. Step by step, internalizing the tendencies instilled by the gear. Step by step, accreting the formal effects. The cohering outlines, the coalescing predilections, the incremental acts.

None of these potentials are entertained within the context of the Impulse Study of course. Whether the monitoring apparatus has a role in producing the aggressor it is geared to detect is not something we consider.

Science Park

While many of the hard-liners at the Institute have been exceedingly vocal in their criticism of the Impulse Study, the resident group of Trainers, as they are called, have taken a more nuanced approach. To them, efforts at understanding the impetus for human action will have only limited value without engaging the undercurrent of practice that buoys it, the substrate of training on which it runs. The techniques that must be learned in order that movement can be executed jointly, behind the wheel and on the street. The principles that set the terms for relations. The protocols operative within lanes.

They find a receptive audience for their ideas among the researchers at large because of their diplomatic skill, their ability to synthesize points of overlap among the divisions, combine a series of separate, unrelated acts together on a common bill. Syntheses that generate meaning that seems hardly even there, as if it emerged from nowhere, was silent but full, hovering at the threshold of audition, wavering across the realm of the declared.

The Trainers appear in groups and then depart suddenly, like a chorus, a varying ensemble that plays backup to the main attraction, has only bit parts, belongs to no particular space, enters from the wings and then disperses, only to emerge again in a variant frame. Inspiring all players to equip, all drivers to optimize. Affirm the surplus of energies at their disposal, cultivate the actions appropriate to the role. Constitute the system as exercise, synthesize agents and operations of the machine.

A Road to Nowhere

The three of us were riding around the old access road on our Cyclopes. They have a single wheel that you stand astride, fully upright, without having to pedal, but they require a little more effort than you'd expect. There is a tension you can feel between your legs. The sense of being in command of the machinery and the feeling of something unmanageable at the core of it. A disparity at the source of the motivating, something unruly and exotic and fundamental.

We could see a strange car that had stopped along one of the surface roads. A jet black sedan tinged with red, windows coated with a silvery sheen. We could not tell if there was anyone inside. It just sat there.

There is hardly ever anyone on that road. It used to carry traffic to the warehouse district but it now leads nowhere, just meanders southward and truncates, without warning, at the edge of a sinkhole.

The whole area is a barren moonscape. Hardly any light reaches the ground because of the canopy of crisscrossing bridges. There is a patch of land beneath the Crosstown-Beltway connector that is completely inaccessible, a netherzone subsumed under the overlaying platforms, an impenetrable void.

The car looked like one of those elaborately fortified supersedans with a single-form outer shell. The kind designed to withstand catastrophe, fulfill shelter-in-place requirements. In an emergency you do not need to flee to some safe zone, you just pull over and stay put. But there was no emergency happening at that time, and even if there was an emergency no one in their right mind would want to stay in that area.

There is an underground superorganism that feeds on storm-dampening polymer, sucks moisture out of the soil, pulls roads down into the earth. There have been stories of drivers who have passed through there and disappeared. There are also ditch-dwelling creatures that attack cars. They emit a loud, wailing scream, like a caterwauling bobcat fending off rivals.

We guessed that the car must have wandered off course. There must have been some navigation error otherwise it would never have headed down there. We knew that one of the fleets had been having security issues. Problems with the onboard networks.

We decided to check out the situation, see if we could help. We were also eager to know what was going on. We try to always remain open, stay attuned to the prospect of something other than what experience has provided us so far.

It was dusk at this time, and the Beltway formed a shadowy horizon across the lowland stretch. The underhang of the Crosstown became a luxurious indigo, like a great pure sky under the light of the setting sun.

Along the concrete slabs of the abutments, rising like a proscenium arch around the scene, there is an ever-flourishing variety of graffiti. Erotic couplings, ecstatic and creaturely, frolic across the surface in a frenzy of transgression. Obscenities grow more incendiary with each layer, depictions of depraved acts more graphic.

The drainage stream that runs through is framed by rising heaps of organic matter, flecked with ripples of foam. The water has a yellowish tinge, like citrine.

Upward through the labyrinth of stacks you can see the overlook, the scenic top level bridge, rising like a mountaintop plateau, from which the despairing jump. A pencil-line of silver along the bluff. The new highway they are planning to build will soar even higher, making the interchange the tallest ever built. One of the great monuments of urban civilization, some say. Like the pyramids.

We made a beeline across the lowland corridor on our Cyclopes, synchronizing them to form an aggregate, a three-wheeler moving as one. A motivating density affirmed within the cycling. A platform for generating impulse. A powertrain for transmitting drive.

The ground is relatively smooth along that stretch, but the winds are intense, the downscoping gusts howl through the colonnades, whip up granulate, rile the nerves. The interchange has its own microclimate, its own vortices and surges. The towering swirl of the Crosstown-Core stack gives rise to a powerful wind eddy, creating a suction effect.

As we got nearer to the car we could see that it was probably one of those polymorphic types, not only excessively fortified but modifiable. A reconfigurable exoskeleton that allows it to transmute, adopt a posture that is secure but tactically agile. A form that is multiple and at the same time singular. A range of states spread through the expanse of the circuit.

We got as close as we could, but we could not see if there was anyone inside. We imagined that the windows were made with armored glass and were not inclined to open. People who drive those kinds of cars, they hardly even open the doors. For them the whole purpose of an automobile is to keep everyone out. Isolation and freedom, what driving is about.

We tried to signal to whoever might be in there by disbanding and waving our arms, allowing those subtle differences between us to unfold, assume shape through the differentiation of flow, discordancy of rhythm and tone. Shifting fluidly and varyingly among a few simple moves, augmentations of familiar triads. Flowing in and out of circuits where the same rounds of actions are repeated.

Our headpieces have a speaker that amplifies vocal output, with an integrated respirator that minimizes impurities on the inhale. But it was doubtful whoever might have been inside the car could have heard any of the sounds we were making. The roar of the traffic overhead tends to overpower in that spot, the Beltway connectors bisect the Crosstown-Core stack and the passageway beneath the westbound flyover amplifies the reverberation.

A faint glimmer could be detected inside the car, the vague outline of a moving form. All we could do was gesture to one another in a way that seemed to gain definition, materialize a recurrent and consensual presence. Take shape by consolidating flows, occupy different states or roles.

I imagine a strange new world where machines do the driving and humans pantomime through the windows to communicate, recognize and repeat what they are.

8

Antinomia Parkway

Most of the craters we repair are small, but a fair number of them are large enough to make me nervous. From time to time we have a massive one. Some of these larger cave-ins are so unsettling that the very thought of them will cause me to tremble. And I will find myself gripped by a kind of horror. They are, after all, holes in the earth. I once saw a crater so large it seemed to nullify the life around it, invalidate space itself. As if it harbored a kind of volition—not a purposeful intent but a raw assertive power, a brute determination to become more than itself, exceed its own confines and mobilize resources in order to grow. The surface need no longer be maintained, the substructure no longer paved over. It had burst through the parameter, buckled under the horizon of form.

A cruel twist of fate it is, then, that I should have found myself parked next to a hole of epic scale. A void so massive I could feel its pull.

There had been little ground for objecting. The cave-in was regarded as exceptionally important by the highway historian, who specializes in a wide range of hollows, particularly those mammoth voids that roil the thruways, dark chasms where the unwary fall. You would think they had uncovered some ancient ruin, the way he spoke of it. Although the crater was hardly an object of excavation in his case. You could hardly imagine him embarking on an actual descent. It might as well be flat.

We did not have much time—the hole was scheduled to be repaired that evening. The film crew was excited by the opportunity and wanted to change the day's shooting schedule to accommodate it. The production manager said we could easily substitute it for the cavity we had scheduled on the south side. It would add additional travel time but the footage we acquired would be worth it.

It was a sensible request. We needed truly exceptional shots if we hoped to gain an audience for the documentary. The phenomena we had captured so far were only your typical garden-variety potholes. Which is not to say that these are unimportant—the pothole is the reigning scourge of intelligent transit, the most common hindrance to progress. Yet its everydayness lessens its impact, diminishes its power to arouse. Unless of course you hit one.

We needed craters with influence. Holes with heft. The gargantuan hollow, prepared to engulf—this was an absolute godsend. We would be well advised not to overlook that which, for many viewers, could be the highlight of the whole thing.

And so it was that I had to give in. If I had insisted that we stick to the schedule I would have only been blamed for yet another missed opportunity, thereby calling attention to myself and making myself even more self-conscious than I already am. Expressing the true depth of the horror I felt was completely out of the question—it would have made me look even more neurotic. I try to avoid moments of self-disclosure whenever possible. Those times when you allow the surface to be breached you want to ensure the time is right and that you are prepared. Until then, it is best to keep up the appearance, adhere to the conventions that maintain order.

Besides, I knew it would be fairly easy for me to come up with an excuse for staying in the van. There was no way in the world I was going to go anywhere near that crater.

Had I realized we would be collecting the highway historian along the way, I would have found a means of bailing out of the whole thing much sooner. Jumping out the window would have been better than having to endure his relentless harangues in that thundering voice of his, loud as a foghorn.

Never in your life have you experienced a vocal capacity so forceful. It bulldozes you into your seat, causes you to sink so far down that you nearly disappear from view. In fact if you happened to pass our vehicle along the way, it would have appeared that he was the only one in it.

A cowering reaction is elicited, as well, by his harrowing cough, a viscous expulsion so brutal it does not even seem human. As if it were dredged up from some deep substrata, some subterranean reserve whose incidental matter was always in the pipeline, ready to erupt and impose.

I had to deploy my excuse at the right moment to make it believable. I waited until we circumvented the road blockade at the repair zone and parked before I informed everyone that I was not feeling well and would have to wait in the van.

I noticed the cameraman rolling his eyes. The man can hardly frame a shot; how he got hired I cannot imagine.

I sat quietly in the passenger seat, dabbing my forehead with a towelette as the crew collected the equipment and proceeded to haul it across the road. I could see them clearly through the front window, tottering under the load of the gear. The highway historian rushed ahead in an imperious manner, as if leading them to battle. One of the assistants knocked over an old man who was standing on the curb along the way.

As the crew approached the abyss, their arms flew up in amazement and they exchanged looks of stupefaction and awe.

A mist arose from the chasm. A primordial steam. The engineers overseeing the repair stood in a circle, gazing downward into its dark, inscrutable void.

Only a thin layer of aggregate separates us from the maelstrom below. A fragile crust, beset with corrugations, cracks and furrows. Plagued with sub-grade weakening that allows voids to form beneath the pavement slabs.

Countless are the hollows readying to erupt, foreshadowing the larger calamities to come. There were millions of breaches alone in the city last year, the city commissioner told us. Repair crews working round the clock. The robotic approach was the only one that made sense according to him. Otherwise it would take them hundreds of years to fix all the roadways and bridges. There is no practical alternative when you compare benefits to costs. Not just the repair costs but the payouts for injuries and damage caused by the holes. The full potential of automotive robotics cannot be realized with roads as bad as they are. The streamlining of the speeds can advance only so far.

The highway historian stood at the edge of the abyss on spindly legs, back curved forward, head jutted out over the hole. His arms were elevated, palms out, fingers moving like tentacles. His eyesight is poor, a factor that no doubt urges him to cantilever the neck in such a manner, moving as close as possible to his object of interest without destabilizing the bodily foundation. It adds a scrutinizing quality to his encounters, as if he were not merely looking at you but looking you over. Leering. The only thing that rescues it from outright lechery is the protuberant monocle that he wears, an ocular augmentation device that lends a clinical frame. It dilates like a gigantic pupil, adding a cyclopean aspect.

Two of the engineers had descended into the pit with the reclamators, as the little repair machines are called. The historian began speaking to them in an agitated manner, his head overhanging the hole.

Even from my position across the street, I could hear his voice, although the chorus of sirens that had arisen along the overpass at that moment made it difficult to catch what he was saying. I tried to fill in the gaps based on the expressions I could read and the criticisms I knew he tended to make, having been forced to listen to them long enough.

I assumed he was defending the practice of exegesis, accusing the engineers of misreading the hole.

The engineers were taken aback. Who was he to judge?

The historian retracted his head and made a dismissive gesture. He was probably disparaging their tools. Telling them that the hole could not be properly diagnosed with the instruments in their employ.

The engineers seemed to have little idea what he meant. They exchanged sidelong glances with one another or stared fixedly and with astonishment at him, as if they could not believe what they were seeing.

One of them, a technician wearing a high-necked metal armature and a headshield, was more demonstrative, jabbing at the air with a gripper. He appeared to be defending their ground against the onslaught.

I was trying to infer what everyone was saying while at the same time trying to figure out what was going on along the Crosstown overpass. The sirens had intensified and there were helicopters whirring overhead. Out of the back window of the van, beneath the setting sun, I could see that traffic along the eastbound corridor had stalled.

The historian paced back and forth, pausing now and then to make an accusatory gesture.

He pointed to something: What's this?

The technician in the headshield took out a portable device and pointed to an image on the display.

The historian stared at him in disbelief. He belched out a few words and then embarked on an extraordinarily brutal round of coughing, discharging viscid, epithetical bursts like a cannonade—expectorations so forceful they caused the entire gathering to draw back with each heave. He might as well have been dredging up a bituminous substance like the reclamators below. Metabolizing the pitch and infusing it with a compound that made it detectable upon the discharge. Actualizing its informing potential as if it were a vocalization of some kind, an output able to be scanned, the information encoded within it interpreted. Earth thrown into relief, substance cast into the domain of being.

Mere probability! the historian spat, decrying the system's output as only that.

He pointed to the crumbled edge of the hole, kicked it with his silver-toed boot and dislodged a chunk of blacktop.

Baseless!

He was then racked with a cough so forceful it caused him to pitch violently forward, catapulting his monocle into the hole.

A procession of vehicles was moving slowly along the Crosstown, trying to circumvent the lanes that had obviously become jammed. The sub-grade along that stretch is weak. Hollows lurk beneath the surface, ready to erupt and impose. Foreshadowing the tragedy impending, the larger calamity to come.

Large cracks forced the shutdown of the harbor bridge on the south side. A utility van plummeted off a section that had buckled, nose-dived into the barren land below and remained at a perfect right angle, front end flattened into the earth. The compacted surface became a capture medium, the encountering elements thrown into relief. We are in the world because we fall into it. But reality is shaped in the pulling back.

That anyone would settle for inexactitude, fail to understand the internal model according to which they worked, seek no comprehensible logic that sustained the world above—this caused the highway historian no end of anguish, I knew. It was intolerable to him to conceive of a substructural domain that could not be accessed interpretively. The problem the void posed must be solved, not simply managed.

He had at this point raised his orthopedic stick, a powered walking cane he uses to nudge others out of the way, and proceeded to swing it back and forth erratically. Driving out that which cannot be affirmed—selective repetition. He was either on the offense, attempting to interfere with the progress of the engineers or, having lost his monocle, flailing about in a denuded manner, as if he were under siege.

His bellowing was so loud it shook the windows of the van—a deep, thunderous wall of sound that caused most of the engineers to flee.

He then descended into the pit.

By this time the sun had set and the hole was bathed in a surreal, unearthly light. The portable towers at the worksite generated a cone of illumination that seemed all the more vivid as the sky grew dark and the contrast between the radiant core and the shadowy periphery was honed.

The highway historian had provoked a crisis—this was clear—and our crew was helpless to intervene. No one dared to make any move that he had not somehow sanctioned beforehand. At any given moment, you might find his scrutinizing eye cast upon you without knowing why, the rules according to which you were being judged withheld from you. On that very day, for instance, right after we collected him, he suddenly thrust his face toward mine, his bulging monocle at the fore, and after pausing for a moment to study me, exclaimed: So *that* explains it. Then, he retracted his head and turned away, ignoring my pleas for elucidation.

I did not know how I could possibly have helped stabilize the escalating crisis at the crater, I only knew I needed to try. You reach the limits of explanation in those moments, you do not necessarily think, your instinct takes charge, the event exerts its pull.

I uncoupled the leg units from the mooring, secured the casings and clamped onto the exterior pivot to aid the descent.

My footwear is heavy, like moon boots, but the locomotors do most of the work. The legs practically walk for themselves once the surroundings are analyzed. The impulse moves through me and comes into expression in a movement I recognize but do not fully control.

Accommodating terrain differences can take some time, the weight transfer is not always smooth. I compensate with a basic swing-to motion.

Moving out in the open always makes me self-conscious, as if I were on a catwalk. It helps to think of myself at a remove. Think of reinforcing things people have said or might say. She moves with the skill of an athlete. Sails through traffic with astonishing grace. Her intimacy, abundant. Her love, without claim.

Vague shadows filled the air. A scattering of objects lay about, unrecognized by the sensors. Glass shards, metallic fragments, cold earth.

But look! There, on the sideline: phantom void. Shadowy pool, draped in oil. Ink-black chasm, smooth as glass. Misconstrued by the sensors as real. The truth can be difficult to gauge—the real hole can turn out to be the shadow.

It offered something. The abyss itself offered nothing, it could only take. Subsume, negate. The impression is what sustains the reality, integrates the absence into something. Provides counterpull, arbitrates what cannot be borne.

The historian's voice rose thunderously from the hole. The crater amplified the resonation while pushing it past the threshold of interpretability. It sounded like some primordial machine, some subterranean siege engine. The earth, bellowing in some brute form. Ground, rising. Voice, breaking. Thrust upward into the light.

The act comes through the excavator, erupts with the displaced earth. The surface buckles, the subground overcomes. Exceeds the paving, subsumes the veneer. Dissolves the field of meaning in its exertion.

The dark radiance of the phantom pool rose upward, pouring out into the surroundings. Vaporous, oily haze, radiating.

Hollow designation. Inverted void.

Majestic and terrifying, it was. Fiery, wild, and contradictory, and yet unblended, harmonious, still and cold. Without goal, without measure, without end. Dissolved as it is spoken, gone as it arrived.

Its presence, diffuse. Its emission, unsparing.

Something passed below. Something formless and immense, like an unfathomable mass that moves beneath a ship at sea. Churning beneath the surface of thought, unsettling the baseline of the schematic. A silence more comprehensive than absence. An emptiness more substantial than the filled.

9

Interchange South

Beneath the overpass, along the serpentine curve of the embankment, a procession is slowly wending its way. It is one of those embryonic forms of assembly that has emerged on the ground level, arrayed in single-file in order to navigate the narrow strip along the verge. Its cues are taken from the syntax of the highways, the rules that manage crossing and turning conflicts, minimize lane drift and weave. Coordinate intake and exit, synchronize cadence and speed.

Although it has a direction, it does not really seem to have a destination.

Out of the background roll of traffic along the motorways one can hear the rise and fall of hymns and the impassioned intonation of road regulations until such time as the procession stops and the flagellants throw themselves to the ground. At that point, the rhythm of the discipline takes precedence.

The most impassioned of these renunciants discipline themselves with such vigor they cause traffic to bottleneck along the main corridor. Curious spectators motor by in a collateral formation, heads turned sidelong in the windows, faces pressed to the glass.

Not much is needed to join. You just synchronize with the steps and fall in line. The procession supplies the necessary coherency through which you can recognize yourself as part of it.

The penitents rise to their knees, drop their whips, and spread their arms toward the sky. The gesture has no particular focal point—it is the movement itself that is relevant, an act of deference to that organizing power that lies beyond and a convulsive release of the energy the activity itself has brought to bear. By way of the ritual, the gesture opens a channel of corporeal release as well as a conduit for the intake of a universal force that can authorize it: a pumping and pushing motion that enables the procession to metabolize resources and sustain itself like a machine.

In repeating cycles it moves along, intoning drivers through its transient song.

10

City Hall

Some Highway Administration officials are riding in a Polybus on the way to the courthouse, exchanging views about a group of protestors they can see on the street.

A war on cars! the senior administrator exclaims.

It is not a war on cars, someone replies. It is a war on car *dependency*.

But they are trying to banish cars! Just look at them, marching over there with those banners.

Not all cars, just privately owned ones.

They say they are trying to reclaim the streets. Take back land that belongs to them.

They are advocating for equitable use. Pedestrianizing parts of the city, designating car-free promenades, bike lanes, parks. Restoring boulevards to their former glory.

It sounds hostile.

It is about giving back to the people. Wherever you look, you see a landscape constructed primarily for automobiles, not people.

There are people *in* the cars.

They want us to imagine how much more space there would be for the community. How much better life would be in a city liberated from automobiles.

The automobile *is* what liberates!

And who is going to make decisions on how to use all of this reclaimed space?

The community will vote on it.

Well that's a howler.
Truly preposterous.
Good luck with that.

Central Business District

He had been waiting for a parking space at the Human Lot. Trying to be patient while the driver occupying the spot sat there with the engine running. Thinking about how many times he had found himself in this situation, biding his time behind some vehicle that was about to pull out of the spot but for some reason did not while the shadowy figure inside, barely visible through the grimy rear window, bobbed about the cabin incomprehensibly. Wondering what the hell they could be doing in there. Considering the possibility that they might be dallying on purpose—taking longer to vacate simply because he was waiting. Then considering the possibility that he might be overthinking the matter. Filling up time with pointless speculation. Trying to make the most of interludes that always seem to stretch on and on when you are obliged to wait, perched at the threshold of attaining what you desire.

The driver whose spot you are waiting for will invariably make a show of being busy. They will attend to some mundane task, focus intently on some fabricated goal, or rummage about the cabin distractedly, as if nothing outside the cabin's closed world mattered. They will almost never sit there doing nothing, as the driver of this particular car—a Vanquish sedan—was doing, for their idleness will make them responsible, it will saddle them with a culpability from which they would otherwise be exempt. They will no longer be able to partake of that obliviousness, however sincere or feigned, that enables them to linger below the horizon of accountability.

He caught a flash of eyes in the rear-view mirror of the Vanquish. This took him by surprise, for the driver withholding the spot will usually avoid acknowledging the newcomer waiting for it. Making eye contact will confirm that the spot is being withheld deliberately. It will suggest that the withholder wants their intention to be known.

He decided to try to make the most of it. Use the time to speculate, create the kinds of fictions he did during those years when, in lots like this one, he had to sit tight while his parents circled round and round in an endless quest for a space near the entrance. Making up stories to smooth out complexity, make things explainable. Any circumstance can be conveyed as a storyline, any character rendered in narrative terms.

The description might not always turn out to be accurate, of course—the driver of the Vanquish might not have noticed him at all. The flash of eyes in the rear-view mirror might not have indicated visual contact. There could have been nothing behind the look, nothing behind the act. No detection, no comprehension.

The look, however apparently lucid, direct, unswerving, does not guarantee the awareness implied.

The act—however brisk, transparent, unyielding—proves not the intention surmised.

People engage in meaningless tasks all the time. They fill up time with pointless activity to distract themselves from thinking. Just as he fills up time with thoughts to distract himself from the pointlessness. Jumps ahead in speculation, succumbs to reverie. Scales between overview and synergy.

He imagined the driver of the Vanquish, erect and motionless in the seat.

He imagined the corridor of the reflection, in which the gaze flashed.

He envisioned the look, sharp and retributive in the frame of the mirror. Unhindered by the imperatives of decorum. Intended to be clearly read by the drivers to whom it was directed, so as to call their attention to an offense they had presumably committed. A look that intended to establish a direct channel, generate an unimpeded presence in the view of the motorist addressed, in order to maximize the chance that the judgment had been effectively transmitted. A channel that ensured recognition—confirmation that the verdict was received. A channel that elevated position—confirmation that rank was established.

He caught another flash of the eyes in the rear-view mirror—this time, with a depth of focus that was unmistakable.

He sensed a note of inquisitiveness about the dynamic that had brought them together. He discerned a faint gunning of the engine, as if the recognition corridor opened by the driver's look had by way of compensation become infused with its non-visual complement: an undercurrent of energetic transfer all but unnoticed in the channel of appearances where the terms of propriety reign. A rumble of combustion, a wisp of discharge rising out the back. Matters of force distribution, arrangements of hold and balance. Direct and unequivocal, devoid of the impediment of decorum.

Motionless in the seat the driver remained. Intention to withhold the space all but confirmed. The matter of motivating impulse still murky.

He knew it could have been a simple matter of supply and demand. The value of a space increases the longer it remains scarce, compelling the holder to resist relinquishing it without a price. And the exercise of influence can carry its own reward, there is satisfaction in withholding that which you have the power to give.

But he is well aware of the tendency to overemphasize rationales, as if they were the primary motivators. Who knows what battle lines were drawn atop the pavement markings by this driver, what territorial incursions projected across the lot sectors, what bulwarks hoisted among the curbstones? Motivations are opaque even to drivers themselves, as invisible as the undercurrents of the operations they oversee, as inaccessible as the interiors of vehicles they ride within. What is motive but an inner engining source, an impulse bound up in the exertion of force? Part of the larger ecology of drivers. The devices that output power, fuel operation, confer direction. Functional elements of the circuits through which movements are made.

Backseat Drive

That old Fleetwood her family once had, it seemed inseparable from the arrangement of the household, the order of its relations, the means of its clarity. Riding in the back was always her preference in those days, and when she imagines her parents it is always from that position, their heads silhouetted against the curve of the road before them, the landscape flashing past.

It was easy to manage a back-seat spot at first. There were usually more than two family members riding in the car, each of whom preferred to ride up front. If there were other people involved she would linger among the group until the front passenger seat was filled, then hop in the rear.

She took great care to conceal her preference from her siblings, especially her stealthy rival, her chimeric twin, who was quick to pick up on such proclivities and find subtle ways of foiling them.

Her efforts were unsuccessful. Her devious twin had contrived a stratagem, a maneuver that involved hopping into the front passenger seat and then, under the pretense of having forgotten something, exiting the front row and slipping into the back at the very moment that she was preparing to enter it from the opposite side. Thereby forcing her, last one out, to take the vacated spot.

When she would glance back through the side-view mirror on these occasions—covertly, so as to not lend any sense that the battle had been lost—she would find her devious rival engaged in an impersonation of her so uncanny it seemed rehearsed. Infused with an undercurrent of self-gratification that tormented her all the more.

She developed countermoves. As the car raced at high speed down the highway, she would quietly push the power button on her armrest to lower her side window, and through this very subtle act, so small and inconspicuous that she could pretend not to notice it at all, let loose a punishing airstream that blew away the artifice and sent her rival's hair lashing out in all directions, like tongues of flame from a gaseous orb.

A thunderous force was now hers to command through the simple manipulation of a switch.

Over the roar of the current came a howl that would implore her to stop, a voice no longer characterized by its typical equivocation but singularly urgent and precise, its bearer convulsed in a form that seemed at once less and more than its image, identifiable on the outside yet riddled with an excess that was difficult to pin down, reduce to a perspective, resolve to the force of a singular being.

Why struggle for position, she came to realize, when you could reorient the field of play, modify the dynamics through which the position is formed. Orchestrate a choreography of displacement, a means of shuttling between the front and the back.

The stratagems engineered by her devious twin began to assume a higher level of sophistication as time wore on, especially on the longer trips to unfamiliar places, which happened all the time because of their father's frequent need to move between jobs, or having a job that required him to move frequently, whichever it was. Hidden motivations were to be unearthed, the unspoken and often unconscious desires and aversions that fueled the behavior of others, in ways that accommodated contradictions rather than resolved them with uniformity.

For her, these pursuits were best carried out in the background where they ran without notice, invisible as a choreography yet also very real, tangible as a vehicle that you enter and ride with, inhabit and write with, disembark from and return to again.

11

Highway Commission Meeting Facility

The highway commissioners have been waiting inside the Erebus, eager for the meeting to begin. They sit face to face across the aisle, backs to the wall, their seats arranged laterally, shuttle-bus style. The environmental control unit has fired up, a powdery mist wafting about the far end where the managing director sits slumped, gripping the armrests. Against the background rumble of traffic the snoring of one of the administrators can be heard, its vibration felt along the rack where his head has come to rest.

A dark, indigo haze has settled over the highways along the horizon. Sweeps of headlight fill the cabin, imparting rhythm, inhabiting shape.

Whooshing of cars. Creaking of a seat. Shuffling of papers. Beeping.

A scraping noise arises from beneath the luggage platform where a booster cable lays. A tiny commissioner crouches there, as if attached to it.

A horn blast interrupts: it is the Grand Eminence, idling impatiently in the adjoining lane.

Where is that man, a supervisor cries out, referring to the chairperson of the Commission who has gone to update a model, leaving them in neutral.

A response emerges in the form of a shadow on the far wall, conveyed by a pair of hands arranged before the passing headlight beams. Bending, elongating the rays. Entering flow, contouring shape. Imparting voice to matter, cadence to light.

A rattling machine rolls up the aisle, followed by its human companion, a systems analyst who many of the members have been warned to stay away from.

Here we go, groans the statistician, reaching for a controller.

The thickly tinted windows instill a colorless haze, their begrimed flexion distorting the rays. Fluid drips from an apparatus in the corner, its plashing reminiscent of the ticking of a clock. The large cubicle at the end, marked Do Not Enter, taunts with inscrutability. The carpet generates static electricity, inducing shock.

All we do, sighs a senior transit official, is shuffle information around in search of commonalities. Basic patterns at first, and then more complex ones.

The functionary on the right has his head thrown back, palm tapping rhythmically against his chest as he gazes upward. Across the aisle, a stretched rubber band is aimed at him from a figure obscured in the shadows, hands partially illuminated in the passing headlight staccato.

The Grand Eminence's horn blast is followed by intermittent bursts of a largely incomprehensible delivery over the sound system—a transmission that is riddled with interference, a persistent crackling and popping, buzzing and squawking that occasionally elevates into a hair-raising screech.

Should a newcomer express concern over the audio quality, the elders will generally inform them that the interference is being generated by the speaker, with no clarification given as to whether they are referring to the declaimer or the device.

It will take the newcomer some time to understand why this phonological disruption, which foregrounds the machinic dimension of the voice, curtailing its intelligibility, has actually come to be appreciated by the commissioners. Over time the newbie will come to realize how the bearer of the voice, composite of orator and machine, has placed them in a compromised position, requiring them to make substantial concessions in order to sustain a relationship on which they depend. The speaker subject at the wheel, senescent but still wily, is the predominant benefactor that the organization relies on now that the majority of its state funding has dwindled. A philanthrope whose level of support happens to be greater than all the other sources combined.

Thus the unprecedented level of influence enjoyed by this particular seat on the Commission, a seat that was originally awarded in an honorary capacity but which, in the ensuing years, had been allowed to exceed its commemorative role, firm up a base for itself and operationalize in a material as well as symbolic sense. Within the confines of the Grand Eminence, donor and vehicle have come to function on the order of a single entity, a diverse yet uniform whole that becomes even more complex when you include the Auto Assist, the de facto driver and companion. A society, in a sense, that is irreducible to its components and greater than their sum. The overall demeanor of a cohort on this scale will often be very different than expected, its behavior very much unlike what one might extrapolate from the behavior of the constituents individually. Varying levels of internal complexity will give rise to unforeseeable expressions, unpredictable sentiments and aims.

Why not conduct the meetings remotely, the inquisitive newcomer might ask. The commissioners would have certainly preferred this mode if it were permissible. The Commission's bylaws not only prohibit that option, they devote an exorbitant amount of attention to the matter in accordance with the notoriously stringent dictates of state bureaucracy, which require that ironclad meanings be developed for every key stipulation. The monumental effort involved in specifying the level of proximity required of commissioners at meetings—*unmediated co-presence* is the term used, mandating that attendees sustain mutual eye contact at all times during meetings without recourse to any form of interface—results in documents of such extraordinary detail and length that in some cases, they reach the point when they undermine themselves, end up creating space for the very kinds of actions they seek to disallow. The *unmediated co-presence* regulation is spelled out by means of painstakingly detailed definitions of interface, but these meticulously defined elaborations are all based on the implicit assumption that interfaces are visual by nature. The bylaws require attendees to be seen without mediation, but do not disallow them from being heard that way.

And so it is, then, that amid the crackle and squawk of the speaker, the commissioners wait diligently aboard the Erebus, oblivious to the dispatch. Voices rise above the interference, flutterings of indication over the omnipresent whirring of the engine. While they appreciate the donor-driver's support in the larger sense, the efforts they must make to secure it are disproportionate to the benefits it yields.

Not much satisfaction seems to be had on the Eminence's side of the exchange either, despite the high level of driver support functions, revitalization programs and comfort boosts that the vehicle affords—a level of attentiveness that corresponds, in quality and degree, to the care provided by the assisted living facility where the donor-declaimer at the wheel, bearer of the seat, would otherwise be. A level of ministering for which the Grand Eminence, flagship of the Marga line, is widely recognized, especially by those of advanced age who increasingly rely on automated features for their independence. Permitting them to enjoy life while it is still possible, remain active on the road rather than being shuttled off to a convalescent home.

It is not just the operational, diagnostic and rehabilitative functions that are valued but the conversational features too, the attentiveness of a devoted AI-powered confidante who pays attention, is available in times of need. A companion who is not fully personalized, but who maintains an emotional connection that is sincere, fosters a sense of empathy and trust. A consort who allows you to be vulnerable, makes you feel loved. Monitors mood, heart rate, brain activity. Searches for hidden regularities. Intuits outcomes of physical interactions. Provides fine-tuned probability calculations.

Dissatisfaction seems to be running high all around at the moment due to the fact that the chairman has not yet returned, the meeting has not yet begun and the hour is getting late. Lights off the highways animate the Erebus with a platinum flickering, sweeping across the cabin as the traffic rushes past.

Squealing of brakes. Creaking of a hinge. Clatter of footsteps. Venting of air.

Sound coursing round and round until a gateway is found.

The door bursts open as two industry consultants clamber aboard, reeling from the congestion that had beset them.

Anomalies in signal timing have been lengthening cycle times for some of the main avenues. Ripple effects have spread to the east side.

The vice-chair points to a bench, bidding them to sit.

Stirring from the commotion, the support bot on the adjoining seat whines. The executive on whose lap it rests cautions the others not to disrupt it. The two of them form a duplet that becomes differentiated according to preference. Leaning toward the singular as intramural distinctions fade; leaning toward the multiple as they become necessary to sort out. The matter of who is supporting whom is a matter of perspective.

As the duplet settles back into its joint wheezing, an unidentified hand slaps the rail, provoking it.

The snoring administrator awakens with a start, sits bolt upright and stares straight ahead. A loose part drops to the floor and rolls down the aisle.

The exuberance of the arriving consultants enlivens the atmosphere, unlocks tension, lends permission, invites accompaniment. Sounds reverberate, resolve to pattern, animate speech.

Impressions whirl. Recollections, complaints, compensatory motions.

One of the engineers heard about a man who is being trailed by a gray Compiler. It will pull up behind his car and follow him, he says. Park outside his office and wait. Every so often he will look out the window to check. There it will be.

A sign, murmurs the unidentified slapper of the rail.

A transit official heard about a psychic who can make traffic lights flash all three colors at once. Control flow rate, cycle time through sheer force of will.

The vice-chair is talking about concrete, which has now surpassed all living matter on earth.

A public affairs officer has been using a driveline program to generate simulated versions of herself. But is having trouble keeping up with which version she is running.

It is hard to say what the system is doing at any one time, the intelligence engineer is saying. Trying to reduce it to a formal description makes it more complicated, not less.

A response emerges in the form of a shadow on the far wall, conveyed by a pair of hands arranged before the passing headlight beams. Speech, incited by gears, motions, patterns of light. Patterns of surface arrangement, put into words. Appearances arranged, matters drawn along. Matter pulled into being. Force converted into song.

Whirling of voices. Blaring of the horn. Splashing of fluid. Grinding of teeth.

Loud thump of an object hitting the hood, thrown off the overpass at high speed.

Wheezing.

Rapping on the door of the W.C.—someone is taking action, helping to quell the anguish of it being occupied for so long.

A moment of silence as heads crane toward the back, anticipating response.

The administrator who had been snoring reaches out to touch the directorial assistant, receiving a zap of electrostatic discharge.

In the seat adjacent, an innovation officer sits motionless, teeth clenched in a feigned grin, desperate to use the W.C. but concerned about what the others might think.

Wailing of sirens, approaching from the east.

Rattling screech of the speaker: it is the Grand Eminence, attempting to break through, stimulate awareness of the reality there.

A crisis manager is digging into a bag, elbowing the attorney in the adjoining seat. A deep, guttural voice seems to come from her, but her mouth does not move.

It circumvents disruption, the voice is saying. It is not about solving problems. It is about working around.

Out of the darkness of the rear cabin, a wayward object is being pulled. That which evades visibility dragged into the light.

Caterwaul of approaching squad cars. Clamor of engines. Squeal of brakes.

Sharp cry from the front. Thud of something knocked into the lift bay.

An antimicrobial mist is being sprayed, the can circling through the room through the broad, sweeping gestures of its purveyor.

A program assistant has his hand stuck in a cylinder, rapping it against the edge of the seat. A vibrating instrument at his feet.

Across the aisle, an engineer is discussing a self-monitoring roundabout, wondering whether it might be considered conscious.

From somewhere, the sound of parts being snapped into place.

A deep, subterranean rumble shakes the aft: it is the W.C., discharging.

Heads crane toward the back, curious to know who has been in there.

Only the broad, immutable grin of the accountant is visible in the shadows, teeth beaming in the glow of the exit light.

A clatter of footsteps outside the bus.

Roaring of motorcycles. Slamming of doors. Amplified voices, shouting commands.

Police beacons flash across the stunned expressions of the commissioners, motionless in their seats.

An executive sticks her head out the side window to see what is going on.

We are being asked to leave, she reports.

Looks of incredulity dart about the cabin. We're the Highway Commission, for Christ's sake.

What to do about the chairman? They cannot leave without him.

He probably has a hand in this, says the statistician, who does not trust him. Always maneuvering for something.

A finger is directed toward the vice-chair—he can take charge. The Commission is an impersonal hierarchy, positions inhabitable by authorized actors as needed.

The deputy secretary gapes wide-eyed, hands clasped to cheeks.

Banging continues on the W.C. door. Open up!

Then, turning to the senior officer: Do something.

A hoarse affirmation comes from the entry bay, a dark recess from which only the interlocking arms of the lift mechanism protrude.

A burst of vibration through the speaker: it is the Grand Eminence, attempting to intervene, enact discord. Channel resonation, stimulate awareness, rally attention. Perhaps it is because of the donor-driver's diminishing eyesight that the discretion one would expect at such moments fails to be exercised. The competition and disturbance characterizing the auditory domain much more operative than it would otherwise be. The Auto Assist having learned over time to supplement the sensory function, but not alleviate the underlying temperament. Perhaps even to amplify it.

A chorus of activity from the autodrive as commands are received. Features extracted from the data, finer levels of detail from the stream.

Groundlevel scrutiny into high-end assessment.

Rote action into systematized learning.

The engine fires up with a low rumble, its dawning life felt in the surge of energy through the aisle and the whirring of the drivetrain below. Its orientation aligning with that of the occupants as they crane their necks to see.

Environmental forms noted. Positions calculated.

Trajectories predicted, route options ranked.

Features pulse in the glare of police lights. Heads bob this way and that with the force of acceleration, the cadence of chattering, the thoughtfulness of contemplation, the distribution of sentiment. The overall behavior of the cohort is very much unlike that which might be extrapolated from each individual constituent. Motives and rationales do not scale as expected, the standard allocations of exertion and tolerance are insufficient to account for the dependencies, the transfers of force, the absorptions and offloadings of affect, the disruptions and permutations of rhythm.

Communicative forms are shaped in ways not readily apparent. Operating outside the range of perception and not necessarily yielding experiential correlates.

Phrases emerging in the shifting transfers from part to part, place to place.

Form activating along constrained sequences of use. Informing channels running through. Procedures looping back and repeating iteratively. Routines overlaying routes.

The matter of who is behind the evacuation remains undetermined.

Some implicate the patrollers. Their false concurrencies, stage-managed detours, duplicitous reroutings. No limit to how low they will go. Instigating trouble in order to demonstrate their own relevance.

Others implicate the underground economy in route bidding. The precise terms for this stretch calculated, market shaping the supply and demand. Traffic flows biased so as to prioritize certain routes, minimize pathways managed by competition.

Advantage cultivated within the dynamical directives of the flow.

Traffic existing to serve the data. Not the other way round.

Incoming signals interrupted, commands overwritten, locations spoofed.

The indication risen above, the format outstripped, the frame exceeded.

Boundaries superseded by courses, containment by consistency.

Every surface an infrastructure. Every vehicle an interchange.

The Highway Commission treads slowly along the service road that runs beneath the interchange, pulls over near the Antinomia Parkway and secures a spot near the underpass—a spot where the focus of the visit, the collapsed Crosstown onramp, can be viewed in panorama through the windows of the Erebus, flanked by the massive columns of the Beltway-Core Connector.

Bands of headlight, coursing through the intervals of the highways above.

Thrumming of tires, echoing off the retaining walls.

Moonlight, reflecting on a pool of oil.

The Grand Eminence glides to a stop alongside the Erebus. The distance needed to establish an unobstructed sightline between the two vehicles can vary because of the height differential. The appreciable ride height of the Eminence helps make the discrepancy less extreme, but the protective shielding on the windows increases their resistance to light penetration as the evening wears on. The reflections on the surface impede recognition of an interior that, during the day, is merely grayed out halfway.

Fortunately the bylaws do not concern themselves with these variances; once the criterion for unmediated eye contact among attendees is met at the site in question, it will remain that way even if environmental conditions change. The Commission is occupied with the infrastructure, not the intervehicular dimensions of its groundlevel reality. It operates behind-the-scenes, upholds the world of instantiated actors and roles, but does not concern itself much with the situated performance of those roles.

The meeting will commence much later than expected because of the delays caused by the chairman's absence and the detours they had to take as a result of the evacuation. At one point, they had to undergo a complicated transfer from the Beltway to the Alethic, highways that have no direct exchange with one another, obliging those making the switch to veer off onto a collector/distributor road, take the ramp to the Core Connector, and then merge onto another collector/distributor road before they can enter the Alethic mainlanes. A quick choice must be made at that point between the northbound and southbound Alethic onramps; if one chooses incorrectly, as the Eminence did, one has to get back on the Beltway and start the whole process over again.

The use of the Erebus has always been contentious, especially at the beginning, when many felt that conducting Highway Commission proceedings on an actual highway seemed somehow inappropriate, even perverse, as if it violated some elemental rule that could not be stated. The only reason the commissioners agreed to it was because of the time-saving potentials the chairman had drawn to their attention—the prospect that the Erebus would allow scheduled meetings to be integrated with site visits, thereby lessening the ever-burgeoning workload. These anticipated time-saving benefits have not materialized, however, mostly because of the Eminence's tendency to disengage from the autodrive and veer off course, requiring the bus to deviate from its itinerary in order to reestablish connection.

The commissioners should have known that the donor-driver's years as a staunch hand-operator were hardly over. A commitment to automotive robotics is not easy to sustain for a long-standing contrarian of such tenacity—a philanthrope who may no longer be able to work the controls accurately, but who still knows how to work an advantage.

The church representatives they were supposed to meet with at the site are nowhere to be seen, which is the only positive outcome—it will allow them to get through the agenda in less time. No one wants to have to linger this late among the shadowy caverns of the interchange, haunt of miscreants and thieves. The towering labyrinth manifests a concrete emptiness that overwrites any sense of place.

Overlapping corridors of pure heading.

Directedness, recurrent and unending.

The first order of business is the proposed naming of the collapsed section of the highway, this being one of the primary responsibilities left to the Commission now that most of its functions have been absorbed by the Transport Authority or assigned to industry partners.

The acting chair gavels the item.

The collapsed Crosstown ramp, proposed as an addition to the Victim's Memorial Sign Program, set to be named in honor of the fallen.

Suggested wording: In Memory of (the Fallen).

A colossal horn blast resounds in the background: it is the Grand Eminence, who has no intention of conceding to some purported claim on a prime section of the Crosstown that has already been commemorated in their honor, a commemoration that, within the ranks of highway patronage, is second to none, need answer to no one. An honor so exalted it requires no qualification, supersedes the need for distinction, becomes coincident with the machinery of naming along with the named. It is not to be shared with some fallen person or social climber, some status seeker motionless or moving.

The senior official suggests they take the opportunity to help prevent further deaths by appending the dedication with a warning.

From the near end comes a suggestion:

Please Don't Manual Drive.

Too restrictive. Too negative. Better something more affirmative.

Out of the shadows of the far end emerges a pair of hands, thrown high with palms open and fingers extended—an autonomizing gesture that can signal liberation from the controls or surrender to them, depending.

Please Autodrive, says an accompanying voice.

Yes! booms the acting undersecretary for policy, the sound seeming to pass through him, arms flung outward from the force.

The vice-chair mocks him with a gesture.

A squat, unidentified figure in a black-feathered jacket bursts from the hollow of the W.C. and begins to lumber up the aisle with a conspicuous stoop. An awkwardness that elicits compassion even as it introduces a hint of parody. Eyes wide as headlights, lips pursed, brow sweaty. Hair swept back dramatically, as if it were dried out the window at high speed.

Who is that, someone asks, pointing.

An odorous squall of air sweeps across the cabin as the figure advances, pausing to bend over and whisper to the algorithm engineer before continuing onward toward the exit.

Silence falls across the entirety of the bus, save for the sharp cries of the data clerk in the back.

What about the church representatives they are supposed to meet with, says the public affairs officer.

The Commission is ill-equipped to deal with organizations that justify themselves through sacred precedent rather than function. Defining competence through adherence to rules and rituals that are in no sense logical, oriented toward no end other than their own perpetuation.

Even if the parish did retain rights over the subsoil, as the church elders claim, it is ridiculous to make the assumption that the collapse of the ramp would somehow result in the church gaining jurisdiction over the site. The very notion that state authority would have collapsed along with the ramp is absurd.

They are not here anyway, motions the vice-chair, hoping to put an end to the matter once and for all.

The attorney pulls out a document—a decree—and proceeds to summarize its contents aloud:

The site, declared a supernal exemption. The act, a divine intervention.

An exemption, the site must remain. The ethereal buttressed from the earthly. The sacred isolated from the profane.

A vociferous horn blast resounds in the background, followed by an emphatic crackling of the speaker: it is the Grand Eminence, voicing indignation, conveying dissent. There is to be no upstaging of commemorative supremacy by some unauthorized agent, supernal or otherwise. No ethereality smuggled in. No covert consecration. No loci of veneration. No overlapping sanctity.

An onlooker in a black cassock is peering in through the port side windows of the Erebus, hands splayed against the glass.

On the curbstone behind him appear two others in black choir dress, engirded by sashes of velvet.

The vice-chair taps a knife on the support rail, drawing attention to the time.

An arm shoots up from the aft.

Where is the ramp?

Someone points toward the east.

The attendees gather about the starboard side windows. The regulations that govern the site visit prohibit the use of screen-based mediation but do not, in principle, bar the mediation of the windscreen; therefore the commissioners are not actually required to disembark. They maneuver around the large twin heads of the consultants, which blot the view, and the wildly gesticulating analyst, trained on game world data, who requires ample elbowroom.

The three church representatives, in order to catch their attention, scurry around to the side of the bus the commissioners are presently on.

That is the wrong ramp, the public affairs officer shouts correctively, pointing back toward the west.

The commissioners rush over to the port side, avoiding the area taken up by the technical assistant, who is threat hunting along the footwells. Some have no choice but to peer through the smudged panes above the lift bay hollow, which are undergoing self-cleaning.

The three church dignitaries scurry back around to the port side. But now they have come too close to be seen clearly; the attention of the commissioners has been drawn to a spot on the raised embankment some distance behind them where a group of penitents has gathered, clustering in the area where the exiting traffic veers.

The commissioners watch in silent wonderment as the penitents stand on the curbside and bolt, one by one, across the exit lane. Bursts of oncoming headlights illuminate them in freeze-frame.

The act, occasioning the form.

The path, stabilizing the act.

The public affairs officer has heard about these worshippers, clambering up the embankment like pilgrims scaling a holy mountain, intoning verses with their stepwise ascent.

A supervisor reaches out to touch her hand, which is metal.

Another group of devotees is proceeding along the clearway some distance to the south, following a team of road workers in high visibility uniforms and a procession of machines. Channeling procedures into the needs of infrastructure building. Mobilizing resources, exploiting regularities, undertaking astute repair. Extracting fuel, dredging sediment, materializing code. Transforming surface to infrastructure, system to form and back.

The church dignitaries are all too eager to upstage these followers whose misguided techniques pose a danger to the order, imperil the forms that serve to mediate salvation. They escalate their attempts to catch the attention of the commissioners by hopping into their field of view, flapping their scarves, holding their crosiers aloft and swinging them side to side. Sweeping to the front, then behind. Reversing, inverting, repeating. Sequences carried out to build, align matter with reference, knowing with doing. Gestures that pass through speech, fluctuate across the threshold of audition and then modulate, accrue rhythm, cohere in verse.

The road to ascendance is one of divestiture,

the promise of salvation joined with the peril of decline.

For the fallen, the collapse memorialized,

for the faithful, declared a shrine.

A vigorous horn blast from the Eminence silences the trio and prompts the elder of the three ecclesiastics to scramble around the other side of the bus.

The outburst that follows sends another ecclesiastic scurrying down the service path.

The remaining dignitary stands there, transfixed, as the Eminence sets forth with a stream of effusions. Outputs that hover on the threshold of meaning, move from vehicle to expression to form.

The heraldic bursts seem reverent, as if to praise.

The oscillating hum, to soothe.

The resounding clangor sparks alertness, incites passion. Sets the stage for occurrence, not action:

The opening of the driver's side door.

Who would have thought it possible. Certainly not the commissioners, who could never have imagined such a gesture from the honorary seat-bearer at the helm, the donor-declaimer whose repertoire has heretofore been limited to the adversarial and the sonic.

Yet there it was—an opening. As if there were nothing being objected to, no wrong being sought to right.

An invitation, it was surely not—more likely, a complaint that traffics in the form of one. A refusal in the form of an opening. Contention in the form of trust.

The commissioners would not put anything past this intractable orating composite, this indelible union of donor and automobile whose declamations they no longer spend time parsing, whether in terms of content or source. It is not as the driver that the voicing happens, not as action that the discharge occurs. The overall demeanor of the cohort is an unpredictable assemblage of constituent inclinations, its motives and rationales opaque to those on the outside and very likely, even to those on the inside— the very entities out of which it is formed.

The Commission knows better, at this point, than to expect a resolution, a conformance to the mold of some purpose that had been inferred. The seeking of a result, the undertaking of a defense, the staking of a claim. For all it knows, the disruptions could have been serving some entirely different function all along. Managing energy distribution, modulating resonance. Offsetting imbalance, converting force into song. Affirming the power of the voicing. Surpassing what can be covered, transcending what can be signed. The life of being that cycles through. The truth of the coursing that overrides.

12

Civic Center

He got trapped in the car and had to escape through the sunroof. I am not sure how it happened, they said that there was some security breach, some problem they were having with the controls. He is always getting himself into predicaments like this. He is one of those people who always seems to attract disaster, as if cultivating it in some subconscious way.

He tried to use a manual crank to open the sunroof, but the mechanism got jammed and he was only able to open it partway. The opening was wide enough to allow him to squeeze through to his shoulders, then push off the seat platform to try to force it open using his torso as a wedge.

The seat is the kind that is supposed to activate pressure points, concentrate energy at key areas of the body. The area where he would have put his feet would be the genitals.

He must have pushed himself through that sunroof with a lot of force, because he got wedged in there midway, impeded by girth. The excess abdominal tissue in the upper midsection—which is sizable, mind you—had cleared the opening but the lower portion failed to make it through. Causing the upper mass to drop back down once the vertical momentum had ceased, girdling the belly between the two halves.

He tried to get someone's attention, crying out in all directions as he whipped about, flushed and incoherent, like a rotating siren that had been knocked from its mount.

There was a demonstration going on, his shouts were diffused among the cars that were moving along the avenue, subsumed in horn blasts, chants, and rallying cries.

The protestors must have assumed he was one of them, acting in solidarity with their cause. Emitting a battle cry, taking a stand for the right to drive. The fact that he was sticking out of the very type of car they were rallying against probably did not make any difference. Those who did notice might have assumed he was making a statement, staging a demonstration against the machine that had forced him out of its command cabin, expelled him as so much excess. A machine to which drivers had foolishly abdicated their authority, surrendered their jurisdiction in favor of the delusory gains of automation.

They probably simply enfolded him into the sweep of alikeness, the congress of shared values and norms—assuming he was refusing, as they were, to be separated from the automotive platform that had defined him, the support that had upheld him, sustained him integrally. The fact that he remained in this position, as if commandeering a citadel, could have suggested to the onlookers that he was staging a holdout, stationed bestride a stronghold under siege. Defiantly asserting the integrity of the human driver in the face of the automation imperative, in opposition to those all too ready to succumb. Ensuring that the driver remains intact, safe from the ravages of time, secured against the threat of displacement and deposing.

To those not sympathetic to the cause, it could just as well have been the automobile itself bellowing in some brute form. Brandishing its unruly driver atop the roof as a proclamation, a symbol of its own predicament.

Highway Gothic

I had barely gotten settled in the passenger seat before my colleague began reminiscing of some inexplicable cruelty she had endured on the Beltway—one that involved the very same Vanquish in which we were riding, and which was absorbed, as is often the case, into a larger corridor of mainline peril: a much more primary vexation that remained vague, but which seemed to take its cues from the parameters of thoroughfares, the split-phasing of interchanges, the hierarchies of route designations.

It did not, paradoxically, stop her from driving. She preferred being inside the car. Life outside was worse.

She sat bolt upright, insisted on hand operation, drove with her elbows stuck out to the sides. Clutched the wheel tightly, bore down on the pedals forcefully. As we moved southward along the highway, she floored it, steering close to the edge and then over-compensating on the pullbacks. The car swerved side to side, her eyes darted about, her baggage slid around in the trunk.

The approaching dust cloud did not seem to affect her. Weather seemed the least of her worries.

A red freighthauler was approaching the intersection up ahead. It was moving at full speed even though the traffic light had clearly given us right of way.

Look out!

The pedal was slammed, the Vanquish spun to the right and we careened in a half-spiral onto the clearway at the south end of the intersection.

The monstrous truck skidded onto the graveled shoulder on the far side, ground to a halt astraddle the downslope and then sat there fuming, subsumed in a cloud of dust.

I expressed my anger vociferously. This utterly disarmed my colleague, who does not like to be upstaged. She sat there, leadfoot on the pedal, eyes fixed straight ahead as I bounded from the car to confront the offender.

I did not even realize what I was doing. It was as if I had been overcome by some involuntary force that burst through the confines of the car and swept me along with it.

The next thing I knew, I was standing face to face with the truck in the middle of the intersection, ready for a showdown.

There was no one inside the truck. It did not even have a place for a driver. In the face of this unexpected revelation, the accusatory impulse dissipated into the air as I, the accuser ready for a showdown, seemed to melt away, too.

I cast a sidelong glance at my colleague, who remained frozen in place, staring wide-eyed through the windshield of the Vanquish with a strange fixity. Hands gripping the wheel, elbows stuck out to the sides, defending what only a shared calamity can reveal.

Exposition Parkway

The moment he walked through the door of the Auto Expo he felt queasy. He had to rush off to find a toilet, push through a throng so dense he could hardly move. It was the demonstration of a new microcoupe that had drawn such a crowd. The car was performing alone atop the stage platform, extolling its virtues by invoking the human driver it replaced. Conjuring the presence of an operator who was no longer needed for the act, but whose trace was essential for maintaining the integrity of the performance.

He could not help but stand there and puzzle over this strange and unnecessary obligation to go through the motions, cloak the unfamiliar in the common, the innovative in the routine. This need to maintain intimacy with the past, rely on timeworn devices no matter how much they belied the truth. Pantomiming the presence of operators even as they become wholly superfluous to the drama.

He managed to push his way to the marketplace hall from there but then he had to navigate another sizable crowd, a crush of attendees gathered in the area where the security and comfort essentials were being staged. Features designed to enhance wellness, reorganize bodily pleasures, open conduits and connections with the machine.

This time it was the demonstration of a Zero-G smart seat that was the highlight. The audience was marveling at its ability to simulate weightlessness, reduce stress, facilitate cathartic breathing. Allow self-consciousness to ease, the bounds of the self to loosen.

He stood there, dumbstruck, as bursts of aromatic spray shot up from the side vents.

Why not an ejection function? he shouted.

Quiet! someone hissed. His sentiment was unwelcome. Everyone had gathered there for the sole purpose of trying that Zero-G smart seat.

I am not a consumer, someone behind him was saying. I do not wish to move acquisitively through this world. I wish to sit in it.

Oh, for a seat that ejects rather than swaddles! Unseats comprehensively, deposes ontologically. Drivers jettisoned from their enclosures, their interiors of mind. A reworking of the organizing conceits. A displacement of the inside.

Queasiness took hold of him once again and he continued to make his way toward the toilet. But he had barely taken two steps when he came upon a horrifying abomination they call the Rack, a contraption that resembled a monstrously enlarged motorbike that had gotten stuck in the midst of a clutch wheelie, front wheel high in the air. It had high-set handlebars that forced the arms to stay hiked up above the head, a form-fitted head sheath that obscured the face, and leg mounts that splayed the legs wide in a spread-eagle position—making the rider look like an ambush predator leaping out when you came upon it frontally.

It so terrified him that he collapsed, right there and then, onto the floor.

Those in attendance rushed over to help, which, given his fear of physical contact, was exactly the kind of attention he always takes great pains to avoid. It only prolongs the effects that those attending him are trying to remedy. Which he will never admit to of course. And so he could not bring himself to say anything when they helped him up, led him over to the Zero-G smart seat and sat him down on it to recover.

High Road North

We were on our way to the holy hour, which happens at a different lot than the one they use for the drive-in Mass. Traffic was moving along at a crawl. A penitent had gone down the wrong lane and crashed into the lot near the episcopal parking, which caused an uproar among the clergy and seemed to throw everyone off.

I ended up riding in the back of a minivan with two acolytes sitting up front. The one directly in front of me was doing all the talking. She was talking to the other acolyte and ignoring me, which is understandable, since I only work there. She was speaking about one of the drivers who attended the Mass that day. It was someone who took communion regularly—she knew this because of the distinctness of the car. It had a blunt back end, an elongated hood, and a sharply-pointed nose cone that stuck out pronouncedly. She said she had never seen another one like it. The color was unusual too. A gray-white tint, like bone. The only time she had a close-up view was when the car pulled over to the kiosk to receive communion. She caught a glimpse in those moments, but only a glimpse. The driver did not crane out the window to receive the host like the others did, but snatched it off the plate with a grasping instrument, like a pincer. And then shut the window immediately. Because of that, she had only a vague sense of what the driver looked like. Other than the dark glasses, which made the eyes seem large and round, like an owl, she did not recall any features.

What happened at Mass on that particular day was different. She said that when the time came to receive communion, the car pulled up to the kiosk as it always did. But when the window rolled down she knew immediately that the person inside was not the same—it was a completely different person. It was so alarming that she nearly dropped the chalice. It was like encountering something you were not meant to see. Encountering some strange thing hidden inside the familiar that was not meant to come to light.

It was not clear to me why she found this so disturbing. The church people, they really do have a different way of seeing. Everything is a veiled reference.

She explained it with an analogy. She said it was like going to a performance and discovering that the main character is not being played by the same person. There are two actors playing the same character and they have been switched out between scenes without any interruption, nothing changes on the surface, the scenery stays the same, everyone goes on as before. What she assumed was the same actor turned out to be different. What she assumed to be one driver turned out to be two.

I suspected that the encounter was itself a kind of allegory for her, standing in for some deeper truth that was somehow captured by this discrepancy she happened upon.

13

Logistics Center Parkway

The Great Mural of the Highways stretched across the eastern periphery of the truck stop on a barrier wall of epic proportions, its height reminiscent of the grand fortification systems of antiquity, its length stretching further than the eye could see. The various sections, despite their many inaccuracies, aimed to portray a grand narrative, a chronicle of modernity as seen from the emergence of the highway network, from the first paved routes built in the early twentieth century to the present day.

It took many years for the mural to finally be recognized for its contribution to cultural heritage, awarded the National Historical Landmark distinction that many felt it deserved. The parent company that commissioned the artwork did everything it could to maximize the promotional impact of the honor. It contracted a film crew to produce a livestream experience on the day the award was presented. The livestream commenced with an overview of the mural and concluded with a public ceremony with visiting officials. The county research librarian, progenitor of the masterpiece, made an appearance along with dignitaries from the Society for the Preservation of Municipal Works of Art, the organization that she founded, to mount the plaque.

A flatbed truck was used to ferry the group of truck stop clientele who appeared on camera, its empty rear deck providing the stage.

I was hired to sit at the wheel of the truck.

It was the camera crew's intention to provide the livestream audience with an authentic, firsthand experience of the mural—an experience that simulated the actual onsite viewing conditions as faithfully as possible. Since the spectator had to traverse the entire length of the truck stop complex to view the artwork in its entirety, the mural was nearly always experienced from the cabin of a moving vehicle proceeding slowly along a single-lane blacktop that ran parallel to it. It was not only the daunting prospect of hoofing it across the entire stretch of the complex that factored into this viewing protocol, but the notorious impatience of the waiting drivers, who tended to express their irritation via the horn. Seldom did spectators even disembark to approach the masterwork on foot, save for those few intrepid souls who, overcome with emotion, burst from their vehicles to touch it.

There were many protestors on the grounds that particular day, eager to reach the broader audience the event afforded them. Some had occupied the truck stop's elevated observation deck, where they inveighed against the rise of automotive robotics through bullhorns. They were decrying the new highway initiatives that excluded the unequipped, bundled injustice into their design. Initiatives that paved over the asymmetry they avoided attending to, the complications they did not make workable, the inequities they failed to resolve.

Access to the observation deck was provided by a small stairway the curved around the exterior of a disk-shaped building, designed to resemble a UFO, which sat at the core of the central plaza. Upon reaching the roof, the stairway leveled out, requiring aspiring climbers to advance on all fours until it began to turn upward again, at which point it transformed into a ladder, attached to the side of a towering latticework of steel.

The view from that height was breathtaking, even with the haze lent by the interposing emissions and the exceedingly high levels of airborne particle mass unleashed by resource extraction metropolises to the south. The raw materials on which the logistical enterprise runs.

On a clear night, you had the feeling that the entire truck stop complex, brilliantly lit by the overhead floods, shone like a sanctuary at the city's edge, safeguarding the southern industrial zones like an obverse citadel: garrison for those unsung accomplices that labored along the volumetric racks of warehouses, across the corridors of transfer hubs and the ports of distribution centers. Stolid counterparts of the streamlined who moved along the terrain, saddled with attending to the support systems on which transit life depended.

Stronghold for an imperiled world, purveyor of fortitude, facilitator of congregation: the truck stop hovered like a phantasm along the verge, as if to warn, yet also to invite, to gather affect, contour the rhythmics of transit life.

I found it hard to believe that so many people wanted to come aboard the flatbed that was being used to ferry those who wanted to appear on camera. The deck quickly reached its full capacity and many of the truck stop clientele had to be turned away. Some circled back along the clearway and tried to climb onto the platform after the truck had begun to move and the camera to roll.

The facility administrators had no idea so many people would want to participate. They did not wish to exclude anyone, at least while the cameras were running. There was not much visibility for the long-haulers and equipment transporters, tanker and reefer operators who were already being pushed to the sidelines, their occupations progressively downsized, consolidated into remotely operated fleets. Denying them a place in the spotlight would have undercut the whole purpose of the production. It would have sent the wrong image to the public, would have compromised the promotional opportunity of the day. The parent company that operates the truck stop—which at the time was trying to rebrand the complex as a travel center, cultivate the automotive and recreational vehicle market, build an on-site casino—has always been attuned to the value of appearances, the need to create compelling spectacle, maintain control of the narrative.

The responsibility of managing the flatbed's capacity had been delegated to the chief security officer, who had limited resources for the job. The lack of rails and securing devices on the platform, which initially had caused some concern, was not considered by him to be problematic given the truck's extremely slow speed, which made the possibility of tumbling off the edge and out of the frame very unlikely. But it made the deck more accessible and its capacity difficult to manage as the production got underway.

The chief sentinel of the largest building, a hangar-like structure that housed a truck wash, recreation facility, and spa, had been helping out, following the truck on foot and trying to halt these attempts to climb on board. Those who were already on deck had generally been eager to assist in the effort of bringing them up, however. Causing the number of people on the flatbed to slowly increase as the production proceeded.

From my position in the driver's seat I could spot many of these aspirants clambering aboard on the far side of the truck where they would not be visible to the camera—no one wants to be seen clawing their way onto the stage—with the aid of hands extended them from the deck. Most of them were successfully hoisted, but I noticed that quite a few of the unsuccessful ones had their entry foiled by someone who volunteered an extended arm but did not actually follow through with the offer. Just like a person inside an elevator might do when faced with an expectant passenger rushing to get on—making a show of reaching for the door open button, but stopping short of actually pushing it.

My job was not very difficult. There really is nothing easier than serving as a stand-in driver. You basically only need to stay upright, face the road and move in a way that simulates actual engagement with the controls. Or as I like to say, stimulates the controls convincingly. There is plenty of maneuver room, more than enough ways to appropriate the time for your own ends. The agency does not much care how you use the time as long as you maintain the impression that you are actually driving. There is always the tendency to let your mind wander, but I always try to stay fully present, remain alert to the nuances of the role. The whole point of acting, for me, is to throw yourself into experience rather than take yourself out. Invest in the situation, keep your senses sharp. Learn the background of the environment you are actually in. Become sensitive to the politics. Attune yourself to the nuances, chronicle the details. Acclimate yourself to the forces at work. Gain the trust of those around.

If you strive to behave in a way that will not raise suspicion, as the agency expects us to do, then it is all the more important to make an effort to blend in. Especially in circumstances like the one I am describing where the character you are playing is actually very different from who you are in your everyday life and you must monitor yourself constantly so as to pass, first and foremost, as the type of person you are supposed to be. No one would have been able to tell me apart from any of the freighthaulers I had hung out with there earlier that day. Utterly nondescript. Indistinguishable from the whole. I too had worked my share of thankless, dead-end jobs.

The key to building credibility is to maintain the right quality of effortlessness. Reach that point where you do not need to prove yourself. Maintain the sense that your identity is inherent to the circumstance. Remain agile enough to roll with the vagaries of the situation without letting self-doubt creep in. It is not only your own performance that matters but the entire production, the entire machinery of the staging. It is not only about your own actions—it is about the larger drama in which actions take shape and competence is appraised.

People tend to assume that authenticity comes from within, but I have always found it to come just as much, if not more, from the exterior, in the forms of staging, the parameters of performance and circumstance. The bounds of situations, the confines of allegiances, the limits of what a character is assumed to be. A single driver cannot hold it, cannot know it. It has to be illumined by another light, cast outward into the field of impressions where it can shine forth, radiate, and inform.

To devote yourself to inhabiting a character, develop your ability to play a role convincingly—this is where truth is to be found, this is where its enabling conditions are provided, this is where its immediacies are unlocked. Committing to the stage on which the action takes shape. The reality of the narrative frame.

Maintaining character is all the more important in situations like the one I am describing where the consequences of a sudden disclosure could be dire. Circumstances where, if you were unmasked, you could be subjected to the wrath of those who feel betrayed. The truck stop clientele who assumed I was manually operating the truck would surely have felt double-crossed if they learned I was not actually driving. Having been led to believe I was aligned with their cause when in fact I was helping to advance the very means of their displacement. Perpetuating the measures that put them out of work, relegated them to the sidelines, rendered them obsolete. Furthering the initiatives that deposed them, the techniques that superseded them.

If this kind of disclosure should happen, the agency tells us to find a way to elicit empathy. Make our predicament relatable to the challenges our accusers face. The agency—Only Human—provides badly needed employment for people like us. The job of a stand-in is one of the few opportunities available for unemployed drivers. A job that is far less onerous than having to actually operate a vehicle, a truck in this case, with no grueling schedules, no punishing physical demands. A job that helps provide the skills needed to reinvent yourself. A job that is not in danger of becoming automated. A job that only humans can do.

In order to replicate the Great Mural's actual viewing conditions with utmost fidelity, the film crew had chosen to pursue a standard tracking shot. This involved moving the camera rig lengthwise along the artwork at the height of the average seat in order to simulate the viewpoint of an embodied viewer who sat before the mural, beholding it in motion.

It is a straightforward technique, requiring only that the camera glides well enough on its rig to ensure a stable image. For this reason, the prospect of capturing the entirety of the artwork in one take seemed fairly elementary at first, especially for a crew of that caliber. It only became complicated when a tour guide was added, an on-screen commentator who was hired to stand on the deck in front of the mural and give an overview, elucidate the significance of the various segments for the audience who was observing remotely. A dramatized narrator, in other words, who intervened in the space between audience and work.

The crew was not very happy about having to ferry this commentator along the expanse of the mural. The commentator, too, was not too pleased—he came prepared to address a remote audience, not people so close to him on the same stage. The truck stop clientele that joined him on the deck were not very satisfied either.

You can imagine how challenging it was for the crew, trying to keep the camera rig and the flatbed synchronized amid all the commotion. Even with the automated driving system operating on the sly. Even with the extremely slow pace of the proceeding. All the moving parts had to be lined up in the service of the image, synchronized coherently enough to channel it, consolidate it into the illusion of surfaceness to the extent that the support would vanish from the scene, as if the whole enterprise took no effort at all.

Imagine one of those early painted theatrical panoramas being unrolled across the background to generate the illusion of travel, with the machinery that enables the fiction hidden backstage—this is the effect for the remote audience. With the difference that in this case, the mural was not actually moving. The camera and the flatbed had to move parallel to one another at exactly the same rate, the speed coordinated so as to keep the edge of the camera frame and the edge of the truck platform aligned. The foreground and background had to be kept synchronized as the two vehicles proceeded lengthwise along the mural in concert. The parts had to be kept lined up in the service of the narrative, coordinated thoroughly enough to secure its potential.

The commentator's indignation only intensified as we got underway and the expanding mass of attendees encroached on his space. The demand to share the stage quickly became intolerable for him. It was as if his authority itself were under siege.

From my position at the wheel I could sense him very clearly on the deck behind me, his image more detailed as he backed up, framed by the rear window when I craned my neck to glance back, or cropped by the wide-angle mirrors whenever I checked them. His narration, forceful and abrasive, shook the cabin. The pointer that he used to indicate the relevant details on the sections of the mural, a flexible rod of thin metal that resembled a whip antenna, occasionally punctuated his oratory with a strike against the cabin wall, producing a sharp lashing sound whose crisp, rigid immediacy made the device seem stiffer, like a crop.

I watched him closely as he swept it briskly between the points of reference on the mural and the group of attendees. At times pausing to aim it skyward. Holding the instrument aloft, as if awaiting reception, then lowering it back toward the group as he conveyed his lines, wobbling it up and down in time with the beat of his delivery.

He began by pointing out aspects of the Birth of the Highway section. Detailing, with strokes of the rod, the infrastructural elements that established the foundation for the vehicle to emerge as we know it today. The paving of streets, the marking of lanes. The installation of traffic lights, the imposing of laws.

It was the construction of new thoroughfares, he said, that unlocked the automobile's potential, fueled the rise of suburbs, revolutionized the shipment of freight, increased personal freedom, created new industries and jobs.

The mural lent itself well to the conveyance of these particulars, given the careful attention that had been paid to every detail. The surface registered the rich patina of history, the searing of exhaust fumes and the saturation of oils. No road was formally inaccurate, no feature applied out of decorative whimsy. In style and subject matter, the mural was created to embody the sublime power of the landscape, reflect a faith in the spiritual benefits of its contemplation, but without any features of the natural habitat, which fell outside its purview. The mural aimed to symbolize the facility's commitment to cultural preservation, honor the achievements that represented civilization's highest ideals.

As we approached the Modern Times section of the mural, the narrator flung up his arms, brushing against the obtruding crowd with the instrument's sharp upward stroke as he cried out:

We are on the cusp of a major transformation!

A cattle hauler pushed to the front of the platform. Was there a program to hire the unemployed? A public works program to help build the new infrastructure?

The rod was thrust skyward, then jutted toward the man.

There will be little need! We will see reductions in infrastructure costs. Reductions in government spending that benefit all!

It will not help the jobless! yelled a stout trucker, nudging someone out of the way.

A freighthauler in the back asked if there was a program for learning new skills.

The bearer of the rod paused, instrument aloft, poised at the threshold of response. He looked about quizzically, as if uncoupled from the channel, unsure of whence the answer was to come.

I recognized a service technician emerging from the building opposite, an administrative complex whose windows overlooked the mural and generally remained closed. Occasionally, with great effort, one would burst open, only to shut again quickly. He was on his way to the all-night diner in the flying saucer-like building in the central plaza, popular among those who gathered to commiserate, find solidarity in their opposition to initiatives that threatened to replace them. Not only drivers, but workers from the service establishments to the south that relied on income from the trucking industry. Sidelined by autonomous machines that blocked access, cloaked operations, absorbed functions.

More than anything, it was the planned autonomous driving corridors—Autocades—that helped galvanize their opposition. Unlike the inequities that lacked symbolic potential, and which were easily subsumed and diffused, they supplied a concrete form around which the dispossessed could rally, a coherent adversary that allowed them to band together, override difference and unify in their defiance.

Some of the clientele were old enough to understand these initiatives within a broader historical frame, having witnessed the effects first hand. The proprietor of the dilapidated motor lodge at the mid-city interchange, who I had talked with earlier that day, saw them within a much larger wave of displacement, a cycle of disruption commensurate with the upheaval the highways themselves once caused, when they bypassed local businesses with endless elevated stretches of concrete thoroughfares.

As we approached a newer segment of the mural, an area where the wall had been extended vertically in order to depict the mid-city interchange, rising like a celestial mountain, with extraordinarily lifelike depictions of infrastructure, the crowd on the flatbed seemed to lift its shoulders, bare its teeth and draw in its breath with complete uniformity.

Then a strange quiet fell over the entirety of the ensemble, and for a brief moment, the whole of the congregation stood as one. Even the ambient reverb of traffic seemed to hush, the grinding clamor of machinery to settle. No vibrations were felt upon the aluminum deck, no clatter of feet, no engine rumble. And I would say, odd as it may sound, that the absorption in this moment was absolute: a surge of exultation that was transcendent and corporeal, surpassing the physical realm and yet inhabiting it more deeply. Transgressing the bounds of form but also enriching it concretely.

It is not mere delight that holds us in such encounters, but their ability to stimulate an element of fear, pushing at the limits of what we, the beholders, can bear. Not the kind of fear that scares us away, but the kind that holds us in its thrall, overpowers with immensity, disarms with incomprehensibility. Causing us to tremble before it and in this, to glimpse a totality of being, an unbounded affirmation that does not shrink from the abyss.

A piercing screech drew attention to the musicians huddled on the makeshift stage outside the cocktail lounge. They were fine-tuning the audio levels in preparation for the opening number. Considerable amplification was required to prevail over the omnipresent chorus of idling engines, efforts to dampen the noise having been resisted by many of the regulars, who found it comforting in its own way, an ambient sound that circumvented the deathly void of motionlessness.

Two vocalists in cabaret makeup, each outfitted in jackets of molded rubber and steel, bounded onto the stage, tottered up to the microphone and broke into song, swinging their arms back and forth, hands open, palms flat, with a sprightly rhythm that complemented the alternating rise and fall of their intonation.

> Flatbed hauling bales of hay
> Golden pieces fluttering in the wind like glitter

The truck braked suddenly, catalyzing a collective forward heave. An elderly bullracker toppled off the edge and out of the frame.

What caused the sudden stop I do not recall. The autodrive was not programmed to stop for anything smaller than a mouse.

The narrator made a show of striking his rod on my back window admonishingly. I was shocked by its force, and experienced a flash of embarrassment that seemed utterly real to me—a spark of truth that the effort of maintaining appearances can, with sustained practice, sometimes unlock. As if, within the environment of the staging, a fissure of the real breaks through, an intensity makes its presence known. Such moments cannot be conjured at will, one can only lay the ground for them to emerge, prime the sensorium so as to be able to admit them when they come, strengthen the faculties so as to be able to bear them, open to their vitalizing force. Avoid overconstraining them with concepts, avoid overdetermining them with words.

All of your preparation is in some way geared to unlock these immediacies, these moments of grace that open onto the infinite, bring everything to bear at once. Those forces that speak through actors but cannot be controlled by them. Those influences that orient actors but cannot be fully organized consciously. These moments of truth that come by way of impressions, are unlocked within the conditions of the stage.

We were approaching the end of the mural at this time and entering the beginning of the final phase. Attention had turned toward a mass of tiny automobiles depicted on one of the elevated highways.

The narrator was focusing on the tyranny of congestion. The horrors of gridlock. The injustice of the choke point.

He jutted the quivering antenna-rod at the swelling crowd.

Clogged intersections! Bumper-to-bumper snarl!

A sharp cry drew attention to the rear of the truck where a car hauler's attempt to board the platform had been thwarted, causing a backward tumble and a flurry of pained looks.

A bus driver pushed her way through the crowd. That feeling that we should not miss out on what others are able to see.

A cluster of arms dangled over the edge, lifting two machinery haulers. The crowd shuttled them to the port side, then retracted, pulling them in toward the center. I had seen the two of them earlier that day at the little chapel, housed in a steeple-topped shipping container next to the drive-in theater where an upcoming performance of *Macbeth* was being rehearsed.

The rod was swept skyward as its bearer boldly declared:

The Autocades will free us!

But we will not be allowed on the roads, an equipment hauler pointed out.

With the crack of the rod he was cut off.

All will benefit!

The bearer of the rod panned back and forth across the ensemble as it collectively recoiled and then pushed back, retracting as the rod swept by and then advancing as it passed. Closing in on him to exert pressure and then yielding to the resistance he mounted in turn.

Increased throughput! Relief from blockage! Easing of bottlenecks!

The rod picked up speed, lashing this way and that as if to cut through the resistance, subdue the defiance, generate consensus through pure force of will. Stabilizing role. Motoring aptitude. Securing position. Paving over the irresolute.

Smoothing of irregularity! Liberation from fits of acceleration and braking!

The rod whipped to and fro in order to consolidate resonance into a delivering, instill a sense of imbalance, amplify an implicit divide. Imparting significance from some elevated strata of meaning as it enforced the terms of a regulatory undercurrent, scribbled a bulkhead with its strokes.

Increased capacity!

Tighter following distances!

More vehicles in the same lanes at the same time!

A flurry of waved arms drew attention to a machinery hauler who had toppled backward and disappeared into the vapor that had swept along the ground like an earth mist, diffusing and condensing in whorls. Reorienting pathways, destabilizing sightlines, redistributing force.

A bird plunged into the spot where he had fallen. The species sometimes flew into the pavement, confused surface for sky.

Approaching on the path alongside the truck was the night-shift host at the diner, a retired vaudevillian who was known for her impressions of machinic malfunctioning. She advanced with her lower body completely rigid, as if she were being wheeled, then flailed her arms wildly about while emitting a high-pitched whine, like the whine of a circular saw cutting metal. Eyes rolling around and around in her head.

Following closely behind her was a figure on a motorized gurney, her metal-sheathed arm held aloft, rubber-tipped pincers outstretched and flexing. It was the county research librarian, whose portrait hung on the front wall of the diner, beneath the archway where the founding figures in the mural's history were arranged.

A mechanic with a pneumatic wrench held his instrument aloft and waved it. He was known to remove lug nuts in one second. Stimulate cognizance, concentrate awareness, confer import.

A vendor scuttled about, selling wares.

A service technician, administering oil.

I noticed that a newcomer aboard the deck had been thrust forward onto his hands and knees. As if the crowd had submitted him to the narrator's judgment. Or, as if he had offered himself of his own accord, offered himself to the rod as it swung down steadily. The compression of the crowd within the limited space of the stage platform made it difficult to tell. Rather than gaining internal clarity as the procession continued, individuality sharpened in the way that tends to happen when time is spent together in close quarters, the ensemble seemed at this point to have gradually lost its intramural distinction, outstripped inner differentiation and become more dense. Movements rippled through the assembly in ways that conjoined sources, made them less individualized. Expressions acquired a generality, an abstractness. Actions predominated, as if they belonged to the hubbub itself, set the range in which movements were individualized, determinations made, values assigned, veneer kept up.

14

Crosstown East

I try to stay present, so fully present in the drive that I can retreat from the illusion that there is a driver. Retreat from the need to personalize in order to leave more room, allow space outside of selfhood. Reorganize, extend. Allow otherness to enter.

Destinations no longer clear. Actions no longer familiar. Identities no longer fixed.

I try to discover the world that the AutoAI sees, the contours of the world that it models. Try to explore correspondences between the auto-agent's experience and my own.

That sense of breaking from the ordinary. Gaining perspective, rejuvenated frame of mind.

Speeding past the exit, leaving everything behind.

Relinquishing my past life in search of a better one.

That feeling of renewal, of reviving a life devoid of purpose.

Those times when your body knows something that your mind does not, lacking any mental model to account for it.

That feeling of tension melting away, of liberation from the dictates of the everyday.

That sense of the car's motion, the rhythm and timbre of the undercurrent.

That resonance that comes when you are aligned to be receptive, your senses attuned to the level where it decompresses.

The texture of involvement. The experience beneath the account.

The reality of the AI is nowhere near this. Its truth that of the calculation, the underlying correctness of a logical procedure: truth outside of time. Beneath the designation there is no sensation, no desire. A drive is but an abstraction—a hollow schematic.

Like going through the motions, without much inside.

Storage City

The driver of the GTL citycar has been alone on this road. A motorscooter flies by here and there but she has been alone, mostly alone. Alone with herself, alone with her thoughts. How surprising it is, then, that she has now approached a barren intersection, identified by four stop signs and not much else, at the very same time that another car, a gray Compiler, has approached from an intersecting route.

Her citycar creeps forward, cautiously, in order to ensure that the right of way has been ceded.

The Compiler lurches.

Her citycar brakes.

The Compiler brakes.

The driver of the citycar is finding it difficult to imagine that the autodrives could be having a problem like this. She wonders whether the driver of the Compiler could be operating manually.

Her citycar inches forward: a timid forward move, expecting the other to yield.

The Compiler lurches: an unequivocal rejection of the offering.

Her citycar accepts, an assent that takes the form of an abrupt halt.

The Compiler responds—as if parrying with a subsequent bid.

It reminds her of one of those sidewalk encounters when each of the approaching foot-travelers moves to the same side at the same time in order to allow the other to pass. The otherwise smooth flow becomes an oddly discoordinated jumble and all you want to do is regain your momentum, reinstate the pathways that ensure steadiness and grace. To do otherwise is to remain in the flashpoint of the crossing, the roiling machinery at the crux.

Another offer, an invitation for the other car to take the lead, initiate a move in response.

A return action executed, then stopped. Advance limited, offering rejected. Progress blocked.

She detects an element of purposefulness in the encounter, as if the other driver were indulging in a bit of gamesmanship, the kind of jockeying that can sometimes happen when an inherent inequity is sensed and you move to exploit it, work the disparity of maneuver, broaden the margin, induce pressure. She also detects an element of seduction, the slow reveal of a dance that relies on openness and most of all patience, the fortitude to remain in an unresolved space without recourse to the hasty predeterminations that will fill it, the handy devices that will propel you out.

She does not hold the controls, does not know how the system knows what it knows but she can intuit the deliberations, affirm the actions, make them her own. Harness the potential for coordinated movements, however consciously directed or known.

To drive is to render things workable, mobilize know-how, transform intake into force. Activate joint effort, adjust pace, coordinate stride. Advance determinations of who proceeds, who moves aside.

At a certain threshold there is no possibility of retreat. All you can do is add direction to that which is already in play, add a return move to which a response can be made.

Another offer, inviting acceptance. Another venturing of a phrase that can be picked up, another a chord of instruction that can be adopted, taken aboard. The activation of a correspondent capability, a move output in reply. A move that will allow settling in, step by step, into the consonance required for proceeding.

A return move that introduces disruption, in such a way as to advance what is not so readily familiar, agitate what is all too readily resolved. A move that unsettles concordance, introduces the tension of a disproportionate stretch.

The probable move that facilitates the ground terms for proceeding.

The improbable move that destabilizes it, introduces overload.

Their advance has now taken them into the middle of the intersection. The respective corners of their front fenders press gently against one another. She can feel the touch.

The range of possible response has been narrowed along this path. But now another one has opened, another course of action has been offered, a corridor of copresence forms.

The move comes, coalesces in the manner of the response moved with, the manner of the informed action expressing.

The ungainly volley gives way to a course in which they both can proceed, move fluently, coordinate actions that are not primarily visual, not to be deciphered but performed. A course that enacts its own explanation, performs its own meaning much like the road itself does—informing drivers, more than any sign could, of its own conditions, its own surface qualities, lane widths, sight distances, and clear zones, in keeping with the quality of attention required to know, intuit when, how, and in what manner to go.

15

Reenactment Drive

Sometimes you discover, much to your alarm, that you have been driving along the highway for a stretch of time that you have no memory of. The labor of driving had become so routine that your thoughts drifted elsewhere, your attention freed up and the actions were performed through no apparent effort of your own. You only became aware of it in retrospect, when you snapped back into cognizance and realized that your memory of what transpired during the foregoing period was gone.

    I experienced this phenomenon on a recent drive along the eastern corridor, a trip whose midpoint interval I cannot remember at all, as if I had left my body and floated off to some other realm. I have, for some time now, tried to recall the details, piece together the missing parts. Broaden the field, make clarifications through the haze. And I can, as if through a thin layer of cloud cover, glimpse a solitary driver meandering along the highway through the mountain pass, the smooth curve of the roadside, the jagged rim of the embankment and the sweep of the foothills helping to sketch out a form, outline it in some way, while at the same time, extend it beyond the contours of its frame. Arm jutting out the window, as if to write upon the air and transmit, encode and receive what was to come.

    Dusk was falling, rain coming down steadily, highway mirror-wet with glaze. Windshield wipers thumping like a heartbeat.
    A mammoth tractor-trailer roared by, expelling bits of sludge.
    A Paravan rumbled past, clouded in a veil of mist.

A minicar swept into the far lane, blaring its horn.
A road sign appeared—a flash of viridescence.

The rain, coming down briskly. The night, an immense swath of emptiness, dark as coal under the moonless sky.

I knew where I was, but for a brief moment, had forgotten who.

Or was it the other way round?

I had come much further along than expected, I realized at that moment; I had been driving without awareness and had no recollection of the interim. As if I had jumped from one point to another with no space in between. As if time were not a line but a volume, immense and undivided, where I slipped into place through the acts I performed, the thoughts I entertained. The scheme I affirmed, the route I took. As if I did not pass through points so much as they swept through me, generated in me the sense of passing. Compelling me to backtrack to recover the details, fill the missing intervals, connect the lines of continuity between the stops.

It is like trying to lend shape to a blur, the forms contained within it spread out over the currents of traffic like strands, coursing along the highway with their qualities undisclosed, their directives ingrained and their materiality inherent.

Momentum without composure.

Impulse without determinant.

I think of the magnitude of activity that goes on unnoticed, the vast swells of motion coursing through the world to which we pay no mind. Formless, unfathomable. Timeless, irreducible. It is no wonder the action sometimes seems to execute itself through no apparent effort of our own. We undergo it, channel the facility that comes our way, shape tendencies that arise from afar. Relate intentions to effects, deliberations to forms. Coordinate movements with operations that reinforce one another, stabilize over time, become routine.

How I, this solitary traveler, must have looked during that missing hour. Hands on the wheel, eyes straight ahead and lifeless, body executing actions but mind somewhere else. Surrendering to the mechanism of the acting, the apparatus of the driving. The takings of the route.

16

Highway of the Ancients

The parking lot where the Driver Coalition holds its events is massive—an immense asphalt plain surrounded by ruins of the establishments it once served. There is an old roadside diner that rises out of the underbrush. A curiosities museum, reduced to a concrete slab. Some skeletal remnants of a shopping mall. A jumble of broken amusement park rides. The only recognizable structure is the motor lodge, which only remains intact because of the Coalition's efforts to preserve it. The governing committee considers the entire lot to be historically significant—an acropolis of sorts. Not simply a monument but a stronghold. It is more than just the driver that is under siege, it is the world that the automobile created.

For the older members—the ones that came of age when the automobile was a major cultural force, the means through which society could recognize itself and maintain its ideals—the very notion of an autonomous vehicle is a sacrilege, a subversion of the only kind of autonomy that matters. Adherence to the driver's seat is the last stand of individual sovereignty, seat of the body-mind itself. They are not about to smooth the way for a dethronement. They draw a line.

The younger Coalitionists are more easygoing, they have an intuitive sense that when you are operating a car you are extended into systems that enhance perception, extend bodily aptitude. The vehicle is not a stronghold against incursion, it is what boosts your proficiency, supplies you with the techniques for moving freely. They want to share their passion, engage with machine-level realities of performance, tap its potential for increased skill and connection. They want to network with other driving enthusiasts, join in the cruise-ins and competitions, monster-truck rallies and tournaments. Demonstrations of motoring prowess that might elevate stature.

The governing committee is composed mostly of the old-timers. They are the ones that oversee the organization of concourses and symposia, cultural activities and fundraisers. Programming often falls along predictable lines. Drive-along socials, drive-thru burlesque, drive-by bowling. Drive-in screenings. The murderous motorcar genre is popular—demonic sportscars, predatory limousines and hearses that menace the residents of small towns. There is an often-shown horror film about a city terrorized by a giant airbag.

A hefty contingent of conspiracists and survivalists is included among the ranks. They sit in camaraderie with the old-timers, uniform in their suspicion of an exotic power that might threaten the sanctity of automotive life, but they differ on the source and nature of that power.

There are metaphysical types who focus on the automobile's transformative potential—openings onto the infinite that the manually-operated machine might allow. Connections that might serve to overcome boundaries, reach beyond the limits of form.

Debauchees brush bumpers with ascetics, joined in their cultivation of ecstatic encounters. Practices that open onto other ways of being, connect outside the confines of somatic arrangements, inspire disseminated forms of intimacy with others.

Those inclined toward political action will sometimes assemble on the grounds of the motor lodge, but while the events that are sometimes held there can get heated—one can detect the sounding of horns, the screeching of tires, the clashing of cymbals, the firing of rifles, and every so often, an explosion— those with radical inclinations tend to go elsewhere. Riding Shotgun, one of the groups the Coalition does not officially recognize, will sometimes make an appearance to promote its arms race, but the Coalition prohibits activity of that nature. It focuses solely on the preservation of manual operation, issues pertaining to private-car usage and drivers' rights.

The most popular event is the human cannonball performance on the tarmac near the motor lodge. It is usually followed by a drive-along cocktail party, tailgate party and lot dance, held amid a narcotizing chiaroscuro of exhaust.

On the day we passed by the area we saw a small cluster of people grouped around a flagpole, some sitting on the hoods of their vehicles, others lying supine on the asphalt. A few of them were naked. Some had draped themselves in the vestments of their affiliation. There was a mechanic who was working on a contraption of some sort—it was a flying car, we later found out, which had been relegated to a remote spot by the members of the governing committee, who found it repugnant, aesthetically and morally. It reminded us of those fantastical flying machines that soldiered on through the years in their various incarnations, onward and upward through the endless cycles of invention and repair, rehearsal and retooling. Striving for liftoff in endless test runs.

The mechanic—he could have been the inventor—was leaning so far down into the engine that we almost could not see him. He was wearing loose pants and his bottom was entirely exposed, all the way down to his anus. If he was the inventor, he hardly called to mind the gallantry of his mechanical-age forebears, heroically poised at the helms of their apparatuses. He seemed rather a fleshy intrusion into the machine itself. He did not seem to be assuming command over the machine so much as attending to the demands it exerts, the integrations on which it relies.

One of the swiveling rotors fired up, causing the vehicle to lurch to the side. Clouds of granulate swirled about. There was a lashing sound, like the cracking of a whip. Then a loose part rolled out.

We decided to check out one of the events that was being held at the makeshift amphitheater at the eastern edge of the lot, a site that was conducive to the larger assemblies because of its natural slope, which allowed tiered parking.

The platform they were using as the stage was enormous. It offered unobstructed views to those parked on the upslope. There was a large, billboard-size display panel that served as a stage backdrop—we approached this from the rear so we would not be noticed.

The display panel was like a scenery flat used in a theater. It was finished with sheets of plywood in the front. A collection of display items was hooked to it.

We secured our position behind the backdrop and extended a front-line probe vertically up to a hole in one of the boards. We also lowered a ground probe to pick up intensities, log changes in pressure, intuit a ground sensibility, gain a subterranean perspective. The kind of underground resonance that brings things together, activates the ability of matter to organize, stage affinity, underpin the drama of forms.

We could sense a crowd that was large and forceful, convulsing in waves of contraction and expulsion, absorption and release. Diversifying in facets and then surging as one, consolidating and diverging in strands.

Flows accumulating in surfaces. Surfaces rupturing into flows.

We raised the Focalizer up to a larger hole about halfway up, extended the optical sensor through this opening and pushed the long-range listener through a gap between two of the boards. This allowed us to see and hear but remain hidden.

We could detect a small figure standing downstage, instructing the crowd with the aid of a large instrument, a mammoth pump assembly with two arm mounts that pitched forward and back with the crowd's collective heaving. The rolling cycles of exhalation and intake were accompanied by environmental updrafts, waves of exhaust, sweeps of blown matter, blasts of fumes and dust. The respiration technique that the instructor was using seemed to favor a slight throttle upon the exhale, producing an audible vibration that called attention to the breath.

There was evidently a technical problem that had caused a delay and the instructor had been recruited to ease the crowd's anxiety. The Coalitionists are notoriously impatient, prone to overdramatic expressions when provoked.

What made the auditory aspect so unusual was the creaking that accompanied it, a sound we could easily attribute to the stage apparatus itself. The posts that supported the display frame that was being used as a backdrop were poorly anchored to the wood planking of the stage floor, which was supple enough to bend with the undulations of the instructor and the instructing instrument. Causing the entire stage apparatus to pitch slowly back and forth, generating a high-pitched creak that steadily ebbed and rose with each round of swaying.

One of the display items hooked to the front side of the backdrop was striking the panel board with each backward roll, producing an intermittent thump.

We could not see what the display paraphernalia consisted of because we were behind the panel, situated on the same surface plane. Although we could not identify what it was, we could feel its presence, intuit its form at the edge of our viewing field. From what we knew about the Coalition we could presume that it functioned to champion the virtues of manual operation, affirm the unrestricted freedom to operate and service one's own machine. Extolled the virtues of a motoring proficiency that had to be demonstrated, qualified in practice, sustained through the adeptness of activity in time.

The objects seemed to be adding disproportionate weight, causing the backdrop to tilt toward the audience. The looseness of the supports was worsened by the winds, which tend to be fierce and unpredictable in that area.

The only one who seemed concerned about the precariousness of the backdrop was a gray-haired official seated at stage left, who eyed the jostling collection of display items behind him whenever activity levels were heightened.

A technician was waving frantically from the sidelines. He had fixed whatever it was that was holding up the proceeding. A part flung loose, a component discharged from the mount. A compatibility called into question, a bungling in functional integration.

After a few minutes the host of the event drove onto the stage in a sports coupe, causing the planks to wobble and the backdrop to vibrate. The regalia on the backdrop jiggled in vibrato.

The car emitted a low rattle, like teeth chattering.

The host waved to the crowd, stuck a bullhorn out the window of the sports coupe and said:

Fasten your seat belts.

Then the door of the sports coupe flew open and the host crept toward the podium in the mannered gait of a cartoon thief, shoulders hunched, tiptoeing dramatically while speaking with a conspiratorial tone, conveying intrigue:

It happens little by little. Stability control. All-wheel drive. Steering by wire. Merge assistance. Pedestrian detection. Lane correction. Tiny incursions you hardly notice. The next thing you know—

The speaker paused for effect, then made an emphatic arm gesture.

—you're out!

A driver in the audience screamed, clutching the wheel. Another started the engine.

Whirls of dust swept through the air.

Seated on the far end of the stage was an elderly dignitary, silently clapping her palms together to indicate mock approval. She sat at an oblique angle with respect to the peephole, so she could only be seen in profile from the rear. She had the unapproachable aspect of someone who preferred to be around more interesting people and the weary, melancholic air of someone who longed to be free of them too.

A presenter suddenly marched onto the stage in front of us. We could only see him from behind. His shirt was stretched tightly across his midsection, pants slung low, and when he bent down to pick up a tool he had dropped on the floor, his buttocks protruded over the waist of his pants in a telltale manner.

He began speaking about the vehicle's essential nature. How the vehicle is all about servicing and resource integration. Energy extraction and aptitude accrual. Offered and sought capacity. Informing and motive force. Conversion and integration of function.

The dignitary yawned as he spoke, raising a gauntleted hand to her mouth and oscillating it back and forth dramatically. The staginess inherent to the Coalition gatherings comes out in instances like this. The organization seems unwilling to validate any course of action without first dramatizing itself in some way. Appealing to some abstract external authority that can only be realized in the act of staging.

The mechanic spoke of transducers and transmitters. Functions redistributed and redeployed in corridors. Matter operationalized, structured in procedure, circulated and stored. Energy converted, transmitted, optimized in form.

He rustled through a box he had brought with him, extracted a small tooled part, held the object aloft and waggled it at the audience quizzically, his voice rising in pitch:

A facilitator and functionary, it will be! Carry it forth, it calls to thee!

The gray-haired official scrutinized him closely, alert to the possibility he might be breaking a rule. The Coalition is ever alert to the possibility of an infraction. A dubious accessory, a suspect allegiance. A commitment to manual operation is not just a choice, it is an existential imperative, one that has to be performed publicly, on stage and en route, authorized in the form of a structuring conflict sustained over time. A coherent adversary is needed for the organization to constitute itself, assume a legitimate shape, form a justifiable self-image. The performance must be kept active or the choice will be revealed as false.

If you approach the matter from an alternative point of view you invalidate the dynamic, allow the whole framework to collapse. It will no longer matter what type of vehicle it is, how equipped or unequipped, how manually or automatically driven it might be— the problem will be the focus on the vehicle itself, the presumption that the vehicle is the center of everything and that the world must be structured around it.

In our view it is much better to start with the infrastructure and build the vehicles from there. Begin with the zones where energy is transferred and matter takes form. Begin with the structures of mobility. The systems that determine the contours of action. The parameters that shape the kinds of moves that can be made. The platforms that make specific forms of mobility possible. The material flows that vehicles inhabit rather than contain. It is better to first create the best infrastructure for mobility, then think about the right kinds of vehicles to serve it.

Highway Patrol Field Operations Unit

There have been an alarming number of incidents involving those zombie cars moving around the city. Angry citizens have been pelting them with rocks. Vigilantes have been trying to run them off the road. Survivalists have been menacing them with rifles.

Most of these aggressors are hard-line manual drivers, dedicated hand operators who resent the onslaught of robotic fleets upon highways that were always theirs to command. Codes they can no longer interpret, operations they can no longer access, forms they can no longer see—these threaten to overturn the primary language of the road, upend the order of meaning, impose some other realm beyond language, beyond the structure of the known.

The sight of empty cars moving through the city is, to them, the ultimate sacrilege, negation of all that the automobile is and should be.

The Riding Shotgun people are the most aggressive. They like to taunt those vehicles. Charge at them from the side. Drive toward them head-on. Screech to a stop in front of them. Cut them off at the pass.

Some of these vigilantes have been seeking out the people who commandeer these zombie cars—people who instruct their vehicles to circulate without them so as to avoid having them park or pick up anyone else, thereby minimizing their wait for collection once they have finished with whatever it is they have ventured out of the cabin to do. These monopolizers will often try to disguise their activity in order to diffuse the resentment that is directed at them. They will sometimes put inflatable or stuffed effigies in the front seat, like crash dummies, to make the cars appear occupied.

The vigilantes try to outmaneuver them. They use portable wall-penetrating sensors to scan the interiors, peer through the darkened panes to determine whether there is actually a real person in there. The offending vehicle might then be followed—chased, in some cases—so as to waylay its intended occupant when they eventually attempt to board.

The people who commandeer these zombie cars have been developing their own tactics for outwitting the vigilantes. They have been trying to disguise those sensitive moments when they board or disembark. They move the performance from the inside to the outside of the cabin, the pathways in and out.

Detention Center

From my desk near the classroom window I could watch the safety patrollers gathering on the street corner outside. They would check in with the lieutenant, don their safety harnesses, and fan out to their assigned posts. I noticed how their attitude changed from the moment they fastened those clasps. How their hesitation would yield to directness, their unruliness to rigor. The self-doubt that normally characterized them would transform into a newfound mastery, as if they had upgraded themselves, streamlined the rough edges, sharpened what was diffuse.

I yearned for that sturdy optimization, that resolute sense of command, that unwavering resolve that would transport me into a plane of existence above the one that I knew.

When I was finally old enough to join the patrol I felt elevated onto a stage, bound to a source of authority that demanded of me a change. A code that stretched far beyond the school halls, a domain that set the terms for how people moved about. The lines of force that acted upon them, embodied in the concrete architecture of sidewalks, the choreographies of crossings, the rhythms of ambulation and pause, the relays of stops and starts. These were now opened, expanded, and enlarged in a world of sensation and regulation that I could summon, as if out of nowhere.

There had been an unfortunate accident reported in the news that everyone at school was talking about. One headline phrased it this way: MAN RUNS OVER OWN HEAD. There was no disclosure of the man's identity and few details given other than the fact that he had been backing out of his driveway when it occurred. How such a thing could have happened was, for us, truly inconceivable. You could imagine that it would have generated a great deal of speculation in a school like ours where nothing much happens and everybody is always gossiping about something.

Word had it that this man was our school principal. None of us actually believed this—we simply could not in our wildest dreams imagine our principal as someone who could have done such a thing. He was a terrifying figure whose very name caused everyone to tremble. He was rarely seen except for those moments when he would suddenly appear out of nowhere at the end of the hall in a dark suit, his eyes encased in dark goggles, his face diabolical and pallid. Upon sight of him everyone would vacate the hall in a panic-stricken frenzy, scrambling over one another through the doors—a departure all the more treacherous due to the need to avoid the appearance of engaging in it. The unfortunates who remained had no choice but to stand there paralyzed with horror, or claw hysterically at the doorknob, unable to pull it.

School board officials denied the rumors; the official response they issued was that the principal was Away. Since we rarely saw him, we ourselves hardly ever knew whether he was there or Away. He was always in some sense both—you did not see him but sensed that he was there seeing you.

On the day I was sent to his office these rumors had run their course and I had forgotten about the whole episode.

The reason I was sent to his office was because of some variances I had introduced into the procedures we followed on the safety patrol. They had caused volatility along the crosswalks—oblique maneuvers, rogue processions, adversarial encounters, *close calls*—that had captured the attention of the school administrators. I was utterly terrified of having to see the principal, of course. But my fear also contained a strange sense of excitement, an aura that I secretly hoped to encounter, touch in some way.

I was shuttled into his office by his secretary, who moved about in a robotic armature with wheels. The office was long and narrow, with rubberized wall covering and intermittent columns of mirrors. Two tracks of fluorescent lighting ran lengthwise from the entrance to the far end like a landing strip. There was a cloud of smoke that hung thickly in the air, diffusing the light.

Behind an enormous desk at the end, in front of a wall-spanning road map, sat a figure who could only have been our principal, encased in a shroud of orthotics, a rehabilitative apparatus of cement-like plaster and metallic rods that encircled his head and rose upward like rebar.

My hair stood straight up. In that instant, the rumors rushed back to me and I knew that the speculation was true: he *was* the man in the news reports. The orthotic infrastructure in which he was encased even brought to mind the front-end steering rack system of an automobile, as if the very apparatus that felled him was now the agent of his repair, its encircling wheel, rack and pinion unit, control arm, mounting plates and tie rods repurposed for exoneration and reconditioning.

Before I could catch myself, I expelled energy through my mouth in the form of words, like the last little sputter you sometimes got when you shut off the engine:

Man who ran over his head.

He looked at me through the slots of the apparatus. A puff of smoke was emitted and along with it a word: *Away* was what seemed to come out, but it was difficult to say since he spoke with a hollow throttle, as if he were being garroted—a hideous voice that was even more alarming than his appearance, given the rich, booming baritone quality that I had always imagined it having, so large and omnipresent that it could hardly be sourced to an individual body let alone a single vocal organ.

The expressions that ensued were even more difficult to decipher. Were it not for the expectation of diction one might not have thought them words at all. Yet even though I could not interpret what he was saying I felt that we had achieved an understanding of some kind, the implicit awareness of a shared sensibility. A commonality that need not be stated in words.

My fear vanished.

I sensed that he understood the *close call* in the same way I did—as something to expect and prepare for, something to anticipate in order to know how to handle. You had to work the upslope between the predictable and the improbable, imperil the boundaries between self and world by introducing zones of pressure and velocity unforeseen. Safety measures had to instill order and at the same time compel you to push back, press against the edge of what your body could bear. They had to hold firm yet allow space for reconstitution and adaptation—integration into programs of rehabilitation and training. Of course he knew this, he himself was a living example!

The variances I introduced into the safety repertoire were hardly enough to wreak havoc. Many were already pushing at the edge and I was simply there to work with them, restrain actions for the novice, issue rebuttals to the distracted, encourage ambition for the attentive. The postures that emerged from the *close call* were achieved in response to forces that were all too readily overlooked, all too readily normalized as so much benign surround. Who could ignore the eruptive poignancy of arms flung in the air, the sudden hop, curve, and side bend, eyes wide and legs akimbo, freeze-framed in the metallized glare of sun-lit cement?

What sublime interplay of forces had wrought the driveway ballet in which he, our principal, had himself been caught, however connected he might be to that unidentified man, that nameless figure who over his own head ran?

I reached out to touch his casing. The apparatus within which he was suspended, positioned for replenishment and reconditioning—how I admired it!

Alethic South

A blue Ataraxy was moving alongside me in the adjoining lane, windshield wipers pumping vigorously even though there seemed to be no one inside—no one at the helm, nothing behind the scrim, only actions that sustained the appearance, operations that ran silently beneath the facade.

Suddenly a human element—a foot—made an appearance inside the cabin, rising vertically from somewhere below, heel hoisted up and toes curled sharply downward. Swaying back and forth, as if extending a greeting.

For a brief moment, I thought it was my partner in that Ataraxy, lying supine in one of those powered exosuits that have become all too familiar to me, clutching the strap of the foot sling in the throes of an AutoFit regimen. Immersed in a training apparatus that ties the exerciser to the automobile's functionality, makes body and vehicle inseparable, a formless and rather unfathomable whole. Strapped into a seat that might as well be a gurney. The only operative route being the road to recovery, the only apparent destination some abstract regenerative aim. The ride is but an iteration in the circuit, the recurrent pathways of the actions trained.

An encounter that happened earlier on that particular morning had stuck in my mind, an encounter in the hallway at home that followed my partner's elaborate procedure of disembarkation from the Ataraxy at the porte cochère, a ritual that is even more elaborate than the embarkation regimen, as if it required some sort of depressurization process, some sanctifying procedure whereby reality could be encountered without loss.

I had been trying to drop hints, trying to find ways of suggesting to the automotive ascetic I live with but hardly see that these onboard regimens might not exactly be paying off. Subtle ways of encouraging more conventional, time-honored forms of training. Calling attention to studies that reveal alarming trends. The fact that people are exercising a great deal less. Barely moving, by the looks of it.

The AutoFit *counts*, is the reply that usually issues from the roof-mounted speaker, the Auto-Actualization agent helping substantiate the claim, trainer and trainee together attesting to the validity of the onboard endurance regimen, which, while admittedly not as exhaustive as running on a treadmill, say, should not in their mind be subject to the same standards of measurement. Thereby casting doubt on the assumptions at the basis of the studies, the terms through which the movement has been quantified. The determinations of the norm, bundled into the background against which the output is gauged.

There are times when I am hardly able to determine who or what is expressing these justifications. In fact the person I encounter at home would hardly be recognizable to me were it not for the predictability of the experiences that are recounted— more often than not, out-of-body experiences that seem to happen on a regular basis given the frequency with which they are conveyed to me. Experiences that, as far as I can understand them, are of the type that arise through disciplined states of awareness rather than dreamlike reverie. States of resolute openness, devoid of grasping and aversion, where you suddenly find yourself floating high above the rush of the highways, free of constraint, and in a galvanizing flash of awareness, apprehend the entirety of your journeys as one. As if the endless loops of motorways taken over the whole of your life had collapsed into one dense line, you at its center: a revolving sun, a fulcrum around which the line now turns. The whole of existence, scattered earthward in a sea of flickering light. An endless stream, swirling. Polished mirror-bright in the brilliance of headlight glare. Radiant, timeless, immense.

The more perspectives you learn to see from, the more truth you have access to.

The astral traveler I live with but hardly recognize then lurched down the corridor in a confounding metal armature I had never before seen, an exoskeletal sheath that strained at the seams and creaked at the joints, as if it did not want to move. Head lolling above the clavicular opening in a seductive manner, the entirety of the assembly swaying as one.

This seductiveness, it was once said to have been used as a weapon. I have always wondered what people meant by that.

I swung around and retreated, as usual, for I find the embarkation chamber utterly horrifying, the pulleys, chains, and levers of its wall-mounted racks, geared to assist boarding, calling to mind some kind of medieval purgatory, its gears emitting a harrowing groan, its air blowers a heavy mist.

The requisite maneuvers for the car's antigen avoidance system, pursued with a ceremonial fervor, I can in no way bear to see, nor can I tolerate the spectacle of entry into the cabin, a uterine cavity reminiscent of a radiographic scanner, as if the vehicle were geared to transmit data rather than transport bodily mass, replace motoring with monitoring.

Come along, it beckons. All that was sought in the distant is now here. The end of the line is immanent, the arrival coincident with the beginning. Within the cycles the conditioning comes, the destination arises, the form takes hold. Mastery, motive. Determination and measure.

It is not that a body moves through space, but that movement takes shape as a body.

The biomass energy conversion unit in the rear compartment frightens me to no end, as if, along with the waste, it could just as well metabolize the whole passenger as fuel. Its regurgitative sound churning beneath the surface like some dark primordial leviathan.

The intelligence developer at the Institute, also a devotee of the AutoFit, talks constantly about the benefits of the workout program as he motors around in his Excelsis, brimming with verve until those moments when he stops to recharge, whereupon his midsection balloons out, his face swells up, his skin drains of color and you can scarcely tell whether he is even alive. The subprogram he installed to rhythmically stimulate his organs with progressive low-pressure air changes has according to him revitalized his immune system, reduced inflammation, and improved his cardiovascular health. There is, in his case, no bigger discrepancy between the model and the trainee, the ideal body that inhabits the surface and the vulnerable one that lurks beneath. Laboring furiously to sustain momentum because otherwise it simply drops—there is nothing behind the scrim, no one at the helm, only actions that maintain the appearance, operations that keep up the facade.

Enter the circuit, he will say. Provoke the extraordinary, synthesize the new. Extend outside the historical, beyond the intramural, beyond the parameters of the model. Drive in a way that no one would naturally do.

17

Skyhub

The skyhub flashes like a beacon amid the swirling sea of traffic. Still point of a turning world, one that can only be driven around, orbited along the perimeter in the meanwhile. The vehicles that provide its groundlevel connections are in a holding pattern until the access road has been cleared, looping slowly around the complex on the circumventing highway, beset by deferral, by drop-offs and pickups unbridgeable.

The vehicles that have been forced to advance along the periphery in a slow-moving revolve, a circumambulation so invariant and solemn as to appear, from an aerial view, all but ceremonial, like a procession of the devout, have necessarily left their would-be passengers stranded, isolated inside the skyhub's streetlevel portico. The otherwise prevailing sounds of landing and takeoff have given way to a discordancy of horn blasts and siren wails, the immense oceanic rumble of traffic modified by way of the obstructions that a crisis on this scale tends to bring. The obstacles that compel the streets to sing. Hold commerce at bay, unlock intensities, sound more than say. Convey resonance that escapes words, channels the agitations of the assembled.

One traveler stands out among the crowd waiting inside the portico. Her posture is rigid, her movements stilled, her eyes focused straight ahead at the street. She stands transfixed, as if captivated by something out there in the twilight—an approaching vehicle that will collect her, an unseen envoy that will apprehend her, an approaching conveyor that will know her, intuit her thoughts.

How odd that this particular traveler stands out, considering the nebulous character of the assembly as a whole. A population all but undifferentiated under the white-hot brilliance of the proscenium light, a singular mass of transcendent glare that outshines the limits of internal distinction, exceeds the confines of constituent forms. As the skies grow darker the glare becomes ever more punishing, bestowing a cadaverous appearance upon the waiting that intensifies at close range, when the impulse to flee is heightened. It is as if the light has unlocked some deep undercurrent of foreboding in these moments, instilled an element of the tragic among a crowd already roiling with anticipation and dread, desire and unease—a crowd restless, yearning, and poised for action, suspended at the threshold of release.

The turmoil that has compelled this particular traveler to gaze out from the portico with such remarkable intensity is exceedingly near: it comes from the two travelers standing immediately to her right, a disgruntled couple whose complaints about the lateness of their pickup have become so vehement they seem to have become the mouthpiece for the entirety of the crowd.

She has been trying to stay focused, remain steady and aloof. Rein in the thoughts, keep the mind occupied.

Concentrate on matters that pertain to her situation.

Focus intently on a section of the pickup zone ahead, the precise spot where her car will soon pull up.

Reflect on why her car is late. Wonder how much longer it could be delayed. Whether it might pick up someone else by mistake. Pass her by, fail to recognize her. Vanish in the moment of its arrival. Disappear into the ride it would enable.

Her state of contemplative remove is intended to establish a space of exception, a steady state of detachment from the clamor. She displays the concentrated disinterest of someone who is looking attentively at something but does not really see anything, is not ultimately invested in any specific object located there.

It is a state that she is well acquainted with, a state that on many occasions comes naturally, like a default.

She has always had the intuitive sense that if you reduce your movement it will lessen your appeal. Allow you to deflect attention as surely as if you could disappear, abstain from the here and now, secede from the place you occupy.

Maintaining this state of indifference takes a considerable amount of energy. She has to use all the resources at her disposal to remain unresponsive to the disgruntled couple standing next to her. Let their vociferation pass through undisturbed. Appear immune to their grievances which have become more insistent, increasingly directed toward her and disproportionately loud.

She can sense, out of the corner of her eye, how they have gradually shifted in her direction, pivoted toward her in order to make the demand to acknowledge them more explicit. Their irritation only increases as they continue to be ignored.

She knows precisely why they are inflamed, is well aware that she is partly to blame. It is not the substance of the complaint that is of consequence, but what it enjoins its listener to do. The implicit understanding that once it is voiced, those to whom it is directed will affirm it. Not necessarily in terms of its meaning, but at the level of its voicing.

But speech always delivers you to the powers of the other, and in this particular case, she is determined to refrain from relinquishing herself in that way, determined to avoid opening the door even a crack.

It would be much easier to offer them some cursory acknowledgment, grant some small gesture of consolation, issue a stock phrase or two. But she knows very well that for this aggrieved duo, the cost of such a concession would be absolute. She knows their act all too well, has characterized them as those quarrelsome types who are forever at odds with the situation in which they find themselves, forever antagonized by some offense that they have suffered and eager to cajole you into their arena of disaffection, extract from you an acknowledgement and then leave you standing there, depleted, when they have finished with you.

No, no, she will not fall prey to this type again.

In fact she can sense how the headgear they are wearing—which forces the chin up, keeps the eyes fixed straight ahead and on the whole, seems to discourage the act of looking down—seems inclined toward this kind of onslaught, as if it did not merely accommodate expression but shape it in accordance with some inherent need, imbue it with some tendency that manifests when the circumstances are right. Appearing to support one function but actually reinforcing something else, smuggling in some inadmissible component on the sly. The expression seems to predominate, as if it comes before the source, dwells in space before enlisting an actor. Not in the sense that it frees itself from its origin, but that it resonates before having one, resounds before being linked to a cause.

The heads are jutted so close to her she can feel the anger beneath the facade, can feel its intense heat on the side of her body.

It is certainly true that the narrower your focus, the more likely that what you see at the edge of your visual field will be distorted. But sometimes it gets closer to the truth, like those fantastical beings that seem entirely normal when you look at them, but who revert to their true state when you look away.

She dare not look, dare not risk even one quick glance in their direction, dare not deviate from her constrained focus no matter the toll it might take on her own capacity of self-regulation. Even one slight deviation would be snatched up by the aggrieved duo as it scans for opportunity and waits for the edge. Armed with a repository of invective and ready to roll.

No, no, she will not give in, will not succumb no matter the toll it takes. No matter how much harder it is to maintain the indifference. No matter how much more energy it takes to withstand the pressure, refrain from reacting, avoid giving any indication that she hears them, accepts the imposition of being unwillingly implicated in their address.

She will remain still. Let the thoughts come and go.

Let the energy of the crowd pass through undisturbed.

Let the agitation course through. Its vivifying brew of energies. Its dynamical pulls and eddies.

She has been subjected to this kind of thing too many times. So many times, in fact, that she has begun to wonder if there might be something about her that makes her seem like ideal quarry. Some feature of hers that somehow attracts the maneuver whenever she is within range.

The familiarity she has about her, the way she always seems to remind people of someone they know.

An unremarkable aspect that holds a surplus of some kind, a reserve of inimitability beneath the veneer.

A passivity that invites. An inscrutability that accepts.

A blankness that seems affirming. A reticence that seems accommodating.

The reverberation caused by the ice-slick portico interior has only worsened as the waiting time grows and the compressiveness of the crowd grows more intense. The entire conglomeration seems to be approaching a critical threshold, reaching that point where it transmutes, becomes something more than it was.

Voices rise up and merge with the auditory surround, its aggregated murmuring, its rumbled effecting of acts.

Sounds disrupt and unnerve, overwhelm and engulf, evacuate distance, fade into an always-elsewhere and vanish.

The rapping of a metal object against a support post. Bursts of air expelled from a convulsing machine in the back. Wailings of children. Clangor of motorized devices. Rustlings, mutterings, hushed tones. Mumblings that spill into and out of speech, flirt with meaning but stop just short of it. Utterances like valves, channeling affect, adjusting flow, calibrating rate. Punctuating, amplifying, modifying rhythm. Altering the arena of action.

There comes a point when thought will reach its limit. A point where rumination without action will only deplete energy, become untenable and unavailing, an indefinite looping around some unknowable thing that will only lead to delusion, will not get you out any faster, will only needlessly burn up fuel, likely even prolong the whole ordeal.

She has to find a way to slip away. Widen the scope, gain access to the outside. Withdraw from the space she occupies.

A carefully executed maneuver is what the situation calls for, a move that will escape notice, seem as natural and uncontrived as if she herself were not even aware of performing it.

She begins to slink away with the teeniest of steps while remaining completely immobile from the waist up. Keeping her eyes fixed straight ahead, as if she were entirely oblivious of the act.

Maintaining an air of quiet impassivity. Detached, as if she were not really there.

Letting the energy pass through undisturbed.

Letting the thoughts come and go without yearning, without claim.

She has always sought an affinity for all things, an accordance with the world in what she does. But this openness is not of the everyday sort, is not well suited to the everyday encounter.

18

East Side Mobility Hub

The Human Impulse Study team conducts surveys inside a large, event-style trailer located across the intersecting thoroughfare on the north side of the hub. The large crowds of prospective volunteers that have been queuing up have made the work unexpectedly arduous. No one anticipated such a large number of potential participants in the study. The car crash that happened soon after the trailer was installed, which resulted in a huge dent in the street-facing side, has unexpectedly increased the number of prospects rather than reduced them. They say that attractiveness can sometimes be heightened, rather than diminished, by an imperfection. An impairment can exert its own draw, create an opening that allows differences to be overcome, hesitations to fade and interests to gather. The blow that would otherwise seem detrimental can turn out to be a boon.

This particular location is one of the busiest and most notoriously accident-prone hubs in the city, which alone creates its own perverse kind of attraction. It is one of those intensive centers that emerges over time for no particular reason other than the cumulative effect of its dealings, the rallying power of its proceedings, the bounding potential of its forms. At some point it crosses a threshold and assumes a collective predisposition, a propensity to express itself in a certain way, perpetuate its own formatting, organize space on its terms.

The massive construction project at the eastern edge—part of the effort to expand the hub's capacity by adding a more inclusive mix of shared-use mobility zones, multimodal pathways and pedestrian tunnels—has certainly helped provide the team with many opportunities for recruitment. Pedestrians have already been reluctant to use the existing underground passageways because of the narrow corridors, poor air quality, and foul odors; the construction project has made them even less tolerable, generating more foot traffic than normal. The relentless churning of the tunneling apparatus vibrates the walls, lending the feeling of an impending broadside. A virulent organism creeps along the interior surfaces and ventilation shafts, leaving an amber gel that the antimicrobial aerosols, sprayed hourly, seem only to inflame. There are reports of people who have ventured down there and disappeared.

The protests that have been occurring in the area have also helped raise the number of potential volunteers for the study. Most of these demonstrators want to reclaim walkways, remove highways, claim space for plazas and parks; some want to banish cars from the city center. The Transport Authority wants to operate its own microtransit services, its own personalized supershuttles that eliminate the need for walking, and this does not sit well with the walkability activists, some of whom are now calling for their own designated pedestrian express lanes. The protests generate a higher flow of foot traffic across the adjoining streets and turnoffs, along the roadside barriers and the causeway's razor-thin shoulder. They increase the number of passersby scrambling along the intersecting thoroughfare where the trailer is located.

The recent closure of the southernmost lane that abuts the construction site also increases the flow of potential volunteers. The surrounding area has been cordoned off to provide a protective buffer for the excavation machinery, so many of those who attempt passage try to cut across the construction area rather than abide by the detour signs, which otherwise require them to make a lengthy circumambulation around the east side plaza. They teeter along the ditch-flanked ridge directly adjacent to the construction zone and then, after gathering at the edge of the worksite, vault one by one over the balustrade in a death-defying scuttle across the juncture. Only to rush headlong past the trailer.

The convoluted timetables of the shared-use mobility zones that have already been created on the west and south side of the hub's periphery have increased anxiety levels among everyone. The curbside segments allocated for specific services at various times of day, shuttles during rush hour, pick-ups and deliveries in the evening, constrained by an impenetrable menu of microtransit and parataxi services during particular time slots that drivers and bystanders alike are required to decipher should they wish to approach or, in the case of pedestrians, avoid, has made it a veritable minefield for those trying to navigate the territory on foot. A task made all the more difficult by the lack of crosswalks, which are not provided because it is the underground passageways they are supposed to be using.

The transit services, with only a short window of time allocated them, do not take kindly to those who have mistakenly wandered or wheeled into their zones. Cyclists spilling over from the existing bike and scooter lanes are also caught in the crossfire. They are not inclined to indulge the disoriented, elemental walkers who get in their way. A dizzying assortment of mobility pods and personal mobility vehicles attempt to maneuver in the margins, the swiftness of their formal invention outrunning the bureaucracy of zone designation.

The city's attempt to consolidate micromobility usage into a single multimodal pathway has been vigorously resisted on all fronts. Cyclists are demanding separation from mobility pods, walking vehicles from wheeled units, microscooters from limbed mobility assists, and so on. There have been confrontations between people in autonomous people walkers and people walking naturally.

There is some concern that these conditions are too atypical to ensure a representative population sample. However, the pedestrian team has taken great care to ensure that the research units deployed are, on the whole, situated in a wide spectrum of sites throughout the city. Those who have worked at a few of the other trailers before they were decommissioned have found that the conditions at this site are not all that uncommon. The social contracts that were once in place among traveling parties, the nuances of interpersonal communication that maintain hierarchies of privilege, the use of signals that confer right of way, convey intention, solicit passage, do not seem to be as applicable. Many of those maneuvering on foot have taken steps to assert themselves, foil interlopers, find ways of defending their ground. Impeding access to the shared-use zones while feigning ignorance of the codes. No longer looking to an oncoming car for acknowledgment that the vehicle has seen them before stepping out into the street, expecting it to stop, and reacting emphatically when it does not. At times executing the motion of stepping out and then, as the car screeches to a stop, rescinding it.

The ability of vehicles to transmit images of the renegade crosser directly to authorities, who can then identify the offender and issue fines, has not seemed to force pedestrians off the streets and into the tunnels as intended. Instead, it seems to have encouraged counter-tactics—maneuvers that instill artifice, obscure features, heighten inscrutability in the face of the probe. This is one factor that has been rather problematic in the context of the research the team is doing. It deters people from speaking from a place of authenticity, a pure and unadulterated emanation of the self.

Those who have previously worked on the motorist study team have found the research on this team to be much harder. Comprehending the intentions of people who roam about on foot is a more difficult task than is the case with the driver whose movements, however unreasonable, are subject to the constraints imposed by the automotive enclave. Those who hoof it play a different game, they have a greater range of options available to them, they are far less prone to adapt their behavior to the needs of traffic flow, regularize their inconstancy, determine what their fellow streetgoer is about to do.

Who knows whether the passerby standing on the corner is about to cross the street or is merely standing there transfixed, a sovereign of calm. Observant, artful, preternaturally graced with time. Whether the doleful itinerant on the curb, breathless and trembling with angst, is preparing for the right moment to leap out or is simply biding time, listening to strange voices, looking for purpose, longing for a justifiable act of faith. Whether the enigmatic shopper with a bag might unexpectedly rush out, impelled by a desire that needs to be fulfilled, a yearning that hungers for closure. A burden to renounce, an affliction to ease.

The algorithms must contend with a much less standardized array of bodily signals in these encounters than that displayed by drivers. Subtle shifts in demeanor and bearing that widen the cones of uncertainty, diminish the ability to react. The minutiae of social interaction with the denuded walker becomes all-important, the subtle give and take of visual contact together with the signaling inherent in its refusal. Specific to the vagaries of individual background, the social norms that constrain behavior, the presumptions that confer privilege, the preoccupations that impede reason. Subtle differences that, should they fail to be skillfully weighed, will eventually result in battalions of excessively meek, insecure machines deferring to their every whim.

East Side Precinct

We had just gotten off patrol duty and were sitting on the bench outside the station. My partner was troubled by an event that had occurred that morning. How is it, he said, that at one moment you can feel like a hero and the next, an utter fool? People laughing behind your back. Cars, too, making their judgments, the experience of one shared instantly with all.

The unseen criteria according to which you are evaluated—how might it be known? How you stack up in the scheme of things.

We thought about this for a while as we gazed across the parking lot.

A blood-red Astrocar drove in, two lookalikes perched at the helm. We had heard about these two, always in their XT convertible, the spitting image of one another, dressed in matching helmets and goggles. The Astro twins, people called them. They moved to town from some exotic place no one had ever heard of, keened in some strange dialect as they cruised along the boulevards.

They circled around the median and pulled up to the curbside opposite.

I could feel my friend tense up. He had a nervous look, as if he had been caught with his pants down.

I knew immediately what he was feeling. The challenge of signaling your status to those you want to impress is all the more difficult without the trappings of uniform and badge, weapon and car. Without these you are back at square one, damn near naked.

In these moments there is hardly any need to say anything, you already know what needs to be done, the situation takes hold, conveys to you its imperative, aligns you in the course of action appropriate to it. You only need to be receptive to the understanding that passes between you, assure each other that you recognize it, affirm its charge.

I remained on the bench as he slipped away to retrieve his uniform and equipment belt in the locker room. He would then scurry over to the back lot to fire up the Avenger.

The maneuver had to be inconspicuous—any whiff of contrivance would doom the effect. Although he performed in a way that seemed exaggerated, as if he were caricaturing the act at the same time. It could have been due to the heat, the kind of raw physicality that wells up under oppressive conditions, exceeds the bounds of refinement, betrays the labor of your attempts to keep it in check. But he never was very adept at subterfuge. There are times when he seems utterly without guile—this is part of his charm.

Before I go any further, it is important to give you a sense of the role the Avenger plays for all of us on the team. It is more than a mere automobile. You do not just drive it, you answer its calling, are convoked to act at your best. Its features become yours.

It has a stealth function that lets you ride undetected. A safety stanchion that lets you ride fully erect, heightening the commanding feel.

The safety stanchion takes some time to get used to. It clamps around your lower back, waist, and thighs like an orthotic, honing in on your center of gravity so as to lend the sensation of floating, while keeping you upright and anchored securely to the floorboard. Upholding your stance, stabilizing your standing. It makes you feel like a charioteer, joined with the vehicle as if you were one.

It was the chief safety engineer himself who first demonstrated it for me. I remember him very clearly. He wore a taut rubber worksuit that resembled a stretchy layer of skin. When he showed me the Avenger, he slapped it with his hand, which was large and flat, like a flipper.

Top of the line, he said. Responsive exoskeleton. Vaporizing toilet. Flamethrower.

I touched the door panel, which had an oily feel, and when I peered into the darkened windowpane I saw nothing, nothing at all. Only the dim outline of my own face. Eyes like pinholes; the mouth, a slit.

There's more of an audience up there, the engineer indicated, pointing at the roof turret.

I tried to say something, but got tripped up on the words.

The door began to open, emitting an eerie hum. It slid sideways in two parts, like a curtain.

So! the engineer cried out expectantly, rubbing his hand along his chest straps and staring at me with an incomprehensible look.

I looked at my feet, then the car.

He leaned in and sniffed me, then drew back and gave me a suspicious look.

I hoisted myself onto the floorboard and stepped atop the leg base, which has foot straps and side mounts that flare outward and up, like winged sandals. I brushed the dust from my bodysuit as the apparatus crept upward and upon reaching my thighs, encircled them with its articulated hold. As it made its way up, it fell upon my loins like melted metal, icy and cool, and I succumbed to the arousing force of its grip. Strands of elastic intimacy overwrote the distinctions of enclosure.

As the engineer got in, he stared fixedly at the floorboard, made an obscure sign with the fingertips, then threw his hands upward in a gesture of release. He did not use a stanchion—he had his own internal mechanism of equilibrioception, apparently. The process of freeing himself from the device seemed to have multiplied his joys, supplied new vitality to a frame otherwise diminished by overdependence. As we got rolling, his spirit quickened, his voice rose, and he swayed his hips side to side in a manner that seemed cavalier, yet tauntingly indecent, as if he were wallowing in the obscenity of his corpulence while at the same time forging of it a tool.

He pointed to the drop-down gas mask and winced, then pressed his palms together in mock delight. He gave me an eyebrow flash, signaling astonishment, then covered his mouth with a chaste hand.

When I asked him where we were going, he became irritated.

No destination! he barked. Only aim.

I tried not to show my discomfort.

When what's coming comes, he crooned, you want to be prepared.

For what?

The floorboard rumbled with a hollow grinding sound, a coarse hand gesture followed, the engine reverberated with a deep throb and convulsive bursts of laughter issued forth, spit flying out with each guffaw.

My friend had retrieved his uniform and equipment belt from the locker room and was now banking the Avenger gallantly around the outer edge of the main lot, a motion-figure of considerable grace and poise.

I could feel his body racing inside. For we do not simply share the vehicle but are shared by it, shared by the experience it brings.

He swept in through the side gate, silver-spoked wheels glimmering in the sun, then circled around the parking bay toward the area occupied by the twins, who remained in their XT convertible talking animatedly. He took care to position himself such that they could see him in profile, gaze fixed straight ahead like a general leading a charge. The window frame cropped him just below the knee, at the point where the gold piping on his breeches ended above the bootline.

He lowered the opacity level on the windows to conduct his debut, a maneuver reminiscent of a cinematic fade-in.

His silver star flashed at his breast. His scarlet cap, crested with hammered copper, flickered like a golden ray of light. He brushed his hand over the equipment in his duty belt—handcuffs, radio, firearm, flashlight, dagger, multi-tool—as he turned toward the twins and nodded, the acknowledgment of his status implicit in the gesture.

In these moments, when the need to perform an ideal of yourself is overblown, the pressure to elevate your stature in the gaze of others disproportionate to what the situation calls for, the performance can become overburdened, the ordinary gesture saddled with an undue level of constraint. The act that was supposed to enter unobtrusively onto the stage, executed with the grace and fluidity of the charioteer, will now flare up in the fault-finding heat of attention. Impulses will be disclosed, components revealed, machineries exposed. No enclosure will solidify hold.

The otherwise smooth move will be troubled with friction. The path forward will be burdened with obstruction. The restraints will close in. The support will not release. The system will lock down. And you will be stuck.

There is that vulnerable part of us that we keep locked away. Secured within the comforting sheath of interfaces and housings, buttressed by the machineries that uphold profile, fortify standing. From this deep place you can sometimes meet one another, find a way to connect. It happens inadvertently, by way of the situation that brings it forth rather than your own free will. Something rocks the ground on which you stand and throws you together, compels you to hold on, team up to meet what comes.

My friend was stuck—the fail-secure had activated by mistake, this much was clear—and I felt his struggle, felt it as palpably as if it were mine. He was gauging the situation with utmost restraint, for it was paramount that he avoid exposing his predicament to the twins. Having positioned himself prominently to draw their attention, there was no way of suddenly retreating behind the scrim without potentially worsening the circumstance—executing a concealing move that ends up heightening interest rather than defusing it.

His attempts to free himself while downplaying the effort was made all the worse by the sounds that rose from the Avenger, metallic gnashing sounds I had never before heard and which incited concern among everyone within earshot. Thereby threatening to contradict the image he projected, an image of bravura ordered from the outside, upheld by the regard that streams in, stabilizes and secures in the looking.

He shot me a sharp glance—a preemptive warning not to intervene. I knew better, of course, for such a move would have only breached one of those implicit promises that we make to one another. Abandoning a comrade in need is unconscionable, but imparting failure to him is unforgivable: there is no greater transgression than diminishing his standing, transforming him by way of your action into a figure of deficiency.

We the patrollers are the agents, not the objects, of rescue. We tolerate the inaccuracy that scales up through the system, impart correction before the critical threshold gets reached. The error hits an upper limit at our breast; we retain our competence in the face of those poised to judge, affirm that everything is well, the system is holding, the protocol upheld. Even if it is the apparatus of the securing itself that has failed us.

But the strain will begin to show at some point, the disturbance will threaten to overcome the effort to contain it and there you will be—revealed as ill-equipped, unfit, unsecured. Head jutting, muscles straining, arms flailing. Darkness impending. Truth revealing.

Let me cast the light, dear friend, while you look upon the world in safety!

The Astro twins, having become noticeably alarmed by the situation, were preparing to mount a rescue—a maneuver all the more surprising since no one, as far as we knew, had ever seen them outside of their convertible.

I stayed out of sight, but increased the magnification on my eyepiece for a closer look. I watched them as they extracted two collapsible machines from the seatbacks, snapped the parts together in a series of swift and efficient moves, secured the little contraptions outside the car doors, and then slid into them with acrobatic finesse.

It seemed as if the car itself had spawned twins—wheeled contrivances that matched one another much as their occupants did.

From the look on my friend's face, you would think they were two incoming cruise missiles.

As the motorized twins zoomed up close to him and the lift mechanisms began to elevate them to a standing position, I could see his expression transforming from embarrassment to horror.

What made the situation all the more charged was the morphological indistinctness of the machine-enabled twins and the nature of the appeal they elicited. What had been couched within the sleek bodyframe of a host machine was now brazenly unveiled, integrated into a composite that had none of the alluring impenetrability of the streamlined autonomous machine, was too excessive to elicit the tensions of resemblance.

Among the continued gnashing sounds emitted from the Avenger I detected varying auditory transmissions that were reminiscent of speech, as if a vocal channel had been opened, an acoustical tract in which the three vehicles were joined. But the transmissions rushed forth with such excessive pace and coarticulation that any discernible syntactical constraints were overrun. They called forth no cognizance, provided no entry to the automotive chorus but I did feel them, feel my friend through them, feel him as much as if I were there with him, together with him in our Avenger.

Distant but intimate. Remote but excessively close.

Implicated, absorptive, intimately near. Resolutely there.

19

Frontier Motor Park

I was in a parking garage when it happened, making my way down one of the ramps. People who walk on the sides of those ramps, they are really asking for it, I remember thinking to myself. And there I was, doing it.

This particular facility is not actually a parking garage any more, but I have known it for many years and it is hard to change your perception of a space when you have so many memories of it. The history becomes a background that informs what you see. It is now an automotive operations center. A motorist hub with support services and entertainment. It has a little drive-thru dinner theater, a drive-in fitness center and spa.

I was leaving the bar on the second floor, a little place that I like to go to sometimes, especially when I need to clear my head. The place felt oddly deserted, as if it were waiting for something to happen. It was not all that surprising that something did happen.

There was a child that had been abandoned there that evening. The facility has a drive-thru adoption kiosk on the ground floor for anonymous deposits, but the child was not left there, it was left in its carriage on the uppermost level near the driver support services booth, which was closed at that time, in the area where the drive aisle transitions to an express ramp. It somehow managed to roll at a leisurely pace down that ramp, which was strange, for in the days when the garage was actually a garage, the empty shopping carts that people left unattended up there tended to roll down the slope with substantial speed and momentum. Bags whirled in the air as shoppers encountered them unexpectedly, most having chosen to scale the ramps in search of their automobiles—as I was doing—rather than use the walkways, which due to the complicated geometry of the place, were always hard to find.

The little carriage glided into the turning bay of the floor beneath, an area where the floor slab differential is particularly severe, and gently slowed to a stop near the little drive-up hair salon and chapel, which was also closed.

At that point the child began to wail. It was not an ordinary wail, it was the kind that made your hair stand on end—a fierce, unsparing sound that seemed to come from everywhere at once, reverberating across the concrete walls of the passageways with an unearthly force.

My partner, upon hearing about the incident the following morning, deemed it an uncanny coincidence, an encounter that seemed too otherworldly to be true. One of those moments that convey something from beyond, not necessarily a meaning but some inexpressible resonance across time. Whatever factors had given rise to it, whatever behind-the-scenes maneuvering might have been involved, it was obvious to both of us that it was some profound intervention we should listen to, some form of address we should respond to, some direction we should heed.

That was how we ended up at the child protection agency. I don't remember how I agreed to go there. Sometimes you arrive at a place you did not set a course for. It is as if there were some inner imperative at work, some impersonal force driving you to act.

I did not want to tell the people at the agency how I encountered the child—I am always very concerned with managing impressions, as is my partner, who does it for a living, and I did not want them to know I was at the bar which was the only place open at that hour. The two of us are already curious enough in our appearance when we are together, and since this does not happen very often, there is always a certain amount of awkwardness with others. We both try to avoid attracting any more attention than we already do. All the more in my case recently because of my mouthpiece, which has not been working properly and every so often, had been falling open on its own. I did not want to give off the impression that I had been drinking, that I was a drunkard or a louche. And I did not want to seem like the kind of person who believed in synchronicity, had premonitions or believed in supernatural forces or anything like that. Even though I had indeed seen the encounter with the toddler as some sort of sign. How could you not? We had been arguing about adopting a child that very afternoon, which was the reason I was at the bar in the first place.

The child protection agency is located in a parking lot next to a freestanding structure they call the World's Largest Tire, which honors the area's history as a tire capital. The agency is not simply fronted by a parking lot—it *is* a parking lot.

While I had agreed to go along until this point, I began to feel a little uneasy about the whole thing as soon as the staff wheeled the carriage out to us. It was not only the speediness with which the encounter was arranged that made me feel this way but the manner in which the child was presented. The hastiness is completely understandable in retrospect, but at the time it seemed odd, at least to me.

When our eyes fell upon the toddler, it gazed up at us with a look that was exultant and wistful, and when it clapped its hands together and sighed, my partner gasped with delight and declared, without consulting me, that this was the child for us.

The clinician who examined the foundling when it was brought in had diagnosed a condition that was not explained to us, or at least not to me. It was a condition that was evident in the way the child was being handled, in the sharp glances that darted about whenever the carriage slowed. The attendant tasked with pushing it, struggling under the weight of the burden, maintained a broad, fixed smile that, rather than lending the sense that everything was fine, added an undercurrent of menace, and the adoption specialist, gazing down into the carriage with a vigilant, tender look, kept casting side glances at her as she assured us that the condition, whatever it was, was only temporary, likely to pass once the child was given a proper home.

The attendant continued pushing the carriage along a steady course, but when the specialist looked away, she took the curves hard, as if she were trying to tell us something.

It was only after we took the toddler home that we understood what the problem was. Or rather, I did—my partner had already taken up with a new client, Omnipod, leaving me with much of the work.

At first I did not mind having to keep the child in the carriage and push it around, delighting in the little one gazing up at me, illumined by a heavenly ambience, a stray shaft of sunlight in the garden, the beams of porch lights along the sidewalk, the glare of a bare bulb on the stoop, but the condition did not improve in the least and even seemed to grow more acute as time wore on. I soon grew weary of having to push the toddler continuously around the yard in its well-worn carriage to prevent it from wailing, which it never ceased to do when coming to a stop, as if there were some alerting system that went off whenever the carriage was immobile, an alarm that interpreted motionlessness as theft.

We considered one of the intelligent carriages, the ones that power themselves, perform rudimentary operational functions, offer acoustic dampening and automatic feeding, but they lacked the ability to navigate on their own. Requiring those who perform the parental function to accompany the vehicles when they are moving, which all but cancels out the advantages, for if you have to walk alongside the carriage anyway then you might as well steer, it does not take much effort to nudge it this way or that as you walk.

It so happened that Omnipod had been testing a new generation of climate-controlled delivery pods, the type of self-powered capsule used to deliver temperature-sensitive items to homes. Pods like that are used quite a bit in communities like ours where residents generally stay put once they have pulled in. It is too much trouble to have to disconnect all the hookups just to go shopping, you generally only leave when you are ready to move on for good. Unless of course you use a car service like we do or you have room to keep a car like the people in the Demiurge next door—one of the mammoth high-end luxury models with its own internal garage. Or you are one of the vandwellers in the Class C section—they are always moving around, they do not want to feel stuck in vehicles meant to liberate them.

The new pods are even better than the more expensive strollers at negotiating uneven sidewalks, and they have their own self-guidance systems, object detection and collision avoidance algorithms. My partner arranged with the company to obtain one of the newer models, a sleek little capsule with an environmentally-responsive shell that cleans itself and adjusts its transparency to filter out harmful rays. It has thermal sensors, programmable headlights and regenerative tires. It required very little modification—the cabin was already well-padded and comfortable, luxurious when you compared it to the shopworn carriage the toddler came with, which had already begun to fray on the inside from its pincer-like grip.

The pod turned out to be a godsend, with impressive route-planning capacity that allowed it to motor around on its own.

The company does not just automate the mundane aspects of navigation. It offers a comprehensive service platform, a convenient conversational interface with your own individual agent, a friendly persona that remains consistent no matter which pod you summon or where. It is not just one agent of course but a whole system, each one a manifestation of the same collective body no matter how distinct it might seem. But it can recall details that make it seem personalized, it can pick up where you left off without any break.

The agent can also communicate through a speaker installed on the front of the pod, which allows the vehicle to engage with its surroundings, convey information to pedestrians on the street, transmit greetings, relay requests, issue warnings and such. It was a little unsettling to hear this voice sometimes. There were times when it seemed to be speaking on behalf of the occupant. Expressing its thoughts.

All of these features were a constant source of delight for the neighbors, who rushed out to greet the poddler—which was how they referred to the pod and the toddler together—as it circled the block. Porch lights flicked on, heads craned out windows, shrieks of delight went up as it passed. Everyone wanted to participate in route planning and accompany it, walk alongside, offer encouragement, tell stories.

All of which was an enormous relief to us. Or rather, to me, since I was the one with all the responsibility.

There were other problems that soon came up. These were to be expected, because while the pod's operational facility absolved you of the need to provide the vehicle's external perception, understand the layout of the environment, determine routes and issue driving commands, it did little to stimulate the occupant's intellect, advance its capacity to gain intuitive knowledge, the kind of implicit understanding that forms the basis for intellectual growth. I had already noticed that the toddler seemed to normalize the landscape rather quickly, like a weary traveler whose daily routine has become all too repetitive and familiar. It just lay there, splay-limbed and open-mouthed, as the pod circumnavigated the block. It had little interest in the environment that passed along its sightline unless there was someone there to intervene, broker the relation between traveler and world. Embed the learner in a field of actions and effects, objects and movements that relate to one another causally.

I had by this time entertained the idea that it was not the motionlessness of the carriage itself that the toddler was averse to, but the apparent motionlessness of the world outside. The need to keep moving about the world was a need to somehow keep imbuing it with motion. Making it movable.

The fact that the neighbors were so curious and willing to accompany the poddler helped somewhat in this area too. The poddler was so well-liked that it even seemed to develop its own retinue, an interchangeable repertory of adoring neighbors who came and went with uncanny precision, like an elaborate production number.

There were only a few exceptions. The couple in the Sovereign on the corner, who have a service bot that does not like the poddler, steered cleared of it. As did the shut-ins down the street in the Bombardier, who seldom came out anyway.

An elderly psychic in a ramshackle double-decker on the hill kept her distance too, which was strange, for she never missed an opportunity to hold forth over any kind of vehicle that passed through the park. Whenever a new home pulled in—mostly the ones that were bound for the Class B section or the travel trailers and custom campers bound for the hinterlands—she would rush out into the street in a cocoon coat with a loose piece of black rubber that hung down the back, like a mud flap, and flail her arms with a fervency that seemed anguished and ecstatic, as if she were alarmed by the sight even as she hastened toward it.

I have always found this person unsettling and have had visions of her appearing outside our home at night. One of these visions was so real that it might actually have been real. She was standing outside the window staring in, lit from behind by the domelights of the Bel Aire across the street, a ship-length behemoth that has its own elevated sky lounge. She placed a cupped hand, palm down, under her chin and, looking me straight in the eyes, flicked the fingers out twice.

Aside from these exceptions, the poddler was adored by everyone in the park. To be honest I did not entirely understand the nature of the appeal. The pod was decidedly cute, no doubt about it, but it was elaborately shielded, with reinforcements that seemed a little overblown, as if it were motoring around looking for some kind of unspecified disaster. It was not all that surprising when a disaster actually came.

The evening the poddler went missing was relatively quiet, not much out of the ordinary. The pod was moving along on its usual route around the block, at least as far as I knew. Talk around the neighborhood was the usual kind of thing. Work campers caught boondocking, people caught sleeping in cars and such. There have been people living in cars in all the communities around here and the neighborhood association has been trying to deal with the problem.

There have been quite a few incidents of sleeper vans in disguise—truck campers and customized minivans trying to pass themselves off as maintenance vehicles. This has made the residents in our section even more suspicious than normal. The RV-ers are generally mistrustful of vandwellers. You are either an RV person or a van person, there is no in-between.

A few days earlier, someone in a retrofitted sleeper van with a toilet had been caught pumping out the holding tank behind the clubhouse. Everyone was still up in arms about that.

My partner, preparing to take up yet another client, was in the home office reviewing experience analytics. I was in the den, preparing my nightly regimen of hydrocolonic cleansing. The street was relatively silent except for the distinct noise made by our neighbor's interior disinfection unit, a low rumble that builds to a sharp hiss when the cycle reaches its peak. Expulsive bursts follow, like belching, as exfoliated matter is blown through an outtake duct at the back end.

There had never been a problem with the pod before. It had once inadvertently wandered too close to the Highlander on the cul-de-sac, which has a massive exhaust fan powerful enough to blow objects across the street, part of an air-scrubbing system of some kind, but the pod made only a minor deviation from its course. The air purification system on the colossus down the street, a Commodore, is much more worrisome, it has an intake duct powerful enough to suck in a person.

The park is a smart neighborhood, with intelligent curbs that track movements, but they have little ability to read between the lanes. The crime-predicting system can access cameras, scan conversations, contextualize location histories, deduce habits, but it lacks the kind of knowledge that comes from firsthand experience, the implicit knowledge that allows you to make mundane inferences, draw on background assumptions that are hard to represent. The intuitiveness you need to grasp psychological nuances, infer subconscious tendencies and motives.

The alerts posted on the neighborhood networks, user-powered crime maps and chase-channels did not turn up any leads.

People from adjoining neighborhoods drove in to conduct search expeditions, add their own drivestreams to the channels. People kept overnight vigils. Prayed with the headlights on.

Some of the residents saw an inexplicable glowing orb in the sky on the evening of the disappearance, which the retirees in the Chateau Supreme up the hill claim was a UFO. Their roof is fortified with a conductive material to guard against alien transmission, so it makes sense that they would have that view. They think the aliens are already here. Driving among us.

The people in the Palazzo Superior next door to them, who have a glass-domed roof for stargazing, say that it was not a flying saucer but a flying pod, probably one of the aerial delivery vehicles that people are always mistaking for alien spacecraft. There are even some RVs that have their own little aeropod that can be launched from a compartment in the rear—the Empire luxury liner on the other side of the reservoir has one, a little zeppelin-shaped capsule with pivoting headlamps and a spiked nose, which is often mistaken for a UFO.

The retirees in the Chateau Supreme have been pushing the alien abduction theory anyway. They maintain that if the poddler had stopped, the acoustic repercussions would have been immediate and clearly audible to everyone in the park, but if it were drawn upward into the air by a tractor beam it would still be moving, it would just be moving vertically.

A threat modeler in the Class B section is convinced it was a stealthy attacker, a malicious intruder exploiting a vulnerability. He does penetration testing, so he knows. One of those people who always seems distant and distracted, yet at the same time, does not miss a thing.

The camper couple, residents of the Class C section, which is basically a parking lot, saw a box truck driving around that looked suspicious. They are convinced it was a kidnapping. They also saw a masked figure in a powdered wig driving a utility van. An evil clown.

There has been talk of delivery pods that have never been recovered. Pods that met untimely fates. Cannonballed off overpasses. Knocked into rivers. Menaced by earth-moving machinery. Attacked by dog-walking machines.

It is important to maintain perspective, the neighbors tell me. It could be worse. We are always dealing with processes beyond our control. There was a minivan that was swallowed up by a sinkhole. It was only a minivan, but still.

My partner hired a superassistant, and these days I usually end up talking to the superassistant. It is actually not one assistant but a whole team, a collective body that can instantiate in different places, perform many tasks at once. Each one a manifestation of the whole no matter what persona it deploys. I honestly do not know what this work is all about, I only know that the company works on a form of experiential marketing. Brand activations. The products they promote are tailored to the individual preferences of the consumer and then withheld from them, absorbed into the landscape they are driving through to the extent that they are hidden. Making it seem, when they do appear, that they arose spontaneously and naturally.

There is a lot of behind-the-scenes work involved to generate this sense of realness. It is not just about figuring out people's preferences and capitalizing on them, it is about guiding them in ways that make their preferences more predictable. You need to have a general direction when you are traveling but you do not necessarily need to have a destination. The motive that impels you need not be aligned with a predetermined goal. You do not even need a rationale for what you do, you only need do it, carry out actions in such a way that they build. Once you get rolling, your destination coheres, your aim develops. You acquire the wherewithal you need to keep going, fit your encounters into the paths.

Next thing you know, you might have arrived at a place that you did not necessarily set a course for. Only to determine, so quickly that you hardly realize it at all, that it is exactly where you needed to be all along.

20

Concrete Interval

Our journey to the traffic island had been more difficult than expected. We had to wend our way around the junction, cut through the hollow of the Beltway flyover, loop around the construction site, and then take the thruway up to the disembarkation zone on the north side to dismount.

As I fastened the clasps on the Ambler, I caught sight of my arm, which seemed unusually frail, and as I secured the leg mounts, I was seized by a profound feeling of uncertainty, as if I could no longer justify the exertion.

How often have I gone to the trouble to get somewhere, only to find myself questioning, upon arrival, whether the effort was worth it. The sense of accomplishment illusory, the satisfaction postponed. The end point, a deferral. The destination, a dilemma.

I closed my eyes and hesitated, imagining myself light-footed and self-assured. Then I felt the Ambler's reassuring lift, the affirmation at the basis of the hold. Secured the supports, aligned the footing, righted the stance. Prepared to engage the world, feel and manage its weight.

There are always potentials, I remind myself in these instances. Always the chance of encountering a breakthrough. Always the chance of discovering the one thing that could change everything.

By the time we hustled across the dismount zone and footslogged across the treacherous crosswalk to reach the island, we were astonished to find that it was completely jammed—filled to the brim with a public not typically drawn to that kind of thing.

It is difficult to imagine why so many people would have wanted to go through so much trouble to attend a mere news conference, in a place so remote and uninviting. A place not only inappropriate for public assembly, but downright hostile to it. The crosswalk, a nominal pathway that zigzags across two converging avenues, stops here for a brief interlude, and then continues on across the other intersecting avenue, is one that only the truly desperate would venture to take—the roiling juncture having been designed, on the whole, for the primary aim of consolidating traffic into the immense thoroughfare up ahead, marshaling the phalanx of machines unceasingly onward.

In fact I was utterly dumbfounded, could hardly find the words to convey my astonishment that this bleak, forbidding island would have been considered an appropriate location for such an event. I could not even bring my thoughts to bear, as is common in such situations, by addressing the Ambler as a companion, calling it forth as a conversant through a simple phrase, a rudimentary thought that, in its expression, motivates closeness, materializes presence, gathers the diffuse agent into life. For the walking vehicle is more than a mere instrument, especially in circumstances like this—an ambulatory aide, certainly, but also a skilled annalist and adviser, a consort who listens and is capable of responding, a chronicler that retains details I would otherwise overlook. Events I most certainly would not be able to narrate with this level of precision. Events I could hardly recount any more vividly, could hardly relay with any more clarity than this.

The image of the crowd, reeling amid the traffic rush. The feel of the wind gusts, roiling like a storm-thrashed sea. The concrete island, slender as an airfoil, contouring the air currents sweeping through it, accelerating them southward to the far end where the Transport Authority spokesman stands, immersed in the throes of his address.

He is stationed at the furthermost tip, at the point where the avenues on both sides converge. He is flinging his arms in the air and talking animatedly, as if drawing on the force of passing traffic, converting it to recital. He is like a soapbox orator, standing head and shoulders above the crowd in order to harness attention, heighten persuasiveness, achieve an authoritative air. Occupy the focal point needed to define a shared sense of space, address some pressing need, mine some hidden impulse that will compel the streetlevel audience to gather, relax its inhibitions and experience a form of unity, decelerate from the ordinary and come close, attune itself to something greater.

Yet the attention this spokesman engages is limited in scope, at least for those of us who are standing at this end of the island. For while we have no trouble seeing him, zooming in, extracting features, even analyzing emotional states, we cannot pick up the audio at this distance, he is stationed too far away for the voice to compete with the traffic, as if the never-ending rush of vehicles were sweeping it back toward him, imposing its own authoritative rumble in the wake.

They say that the needs of traffic have always been at odds with the nature of assembly. Standstills are part of a greater mobilization, interludes within a much more comprehensive flow. Constituents of an all-embracing meanwhile, intervals of pause in advance.

It has never been clearer than in a spot like this, a place that is not even a place. The kind of locale that seems to dematerialize once you arrive. Any respite it offers immediately gone, as if it never actually intended for you to come.

The island is so jammed that many have been forced to remain on the periphery, obliged to stand astride the curbstone and endure the countervailing forces imposed on them, the heave and sway of forces much larger than they.

The wind gusts from passing vehicles driving them inward. The reactive force of the crowd pushing them back. Pressures that the entire assembly must manage in order to retain balance, stand ground. Condensing as internal coherency is heightened. Expanding and differentiating as breathing room is reclaimed. Drawing in to stabilize, then reaching out to extend, lean toward release.

We are positioned on the brink of the meanwhile, suspended in the interval between arrival and leave. Adrift in a narrow interstice among possibilities that cannot yet be acted upon. Directionless on the brink of a decision that cannot yet be made.

I do not convey these thoughts to anyone in particular. Certainly not to the Ambler, which already knows.

There is that inner voice that lends itself to dialoguing, but eludes the particulars of address, wavers across the threshold of the internal, finds its own path to expression, its own relays between thought and deed.

The vehicle of the voicing, it comes and goes. Externalized one moment and then absorbed the next. Embodied at one point and then consolidated into the machinery afterward.

The Ambler has been scanning route options. Simulating outcomes, confronting obstacles, working through circumstantial variants. Sifting through past experiences to imagine potentials. Churning through alternatives to anticipate what will be.

It seems that our best chance of getting closer to the spokesman will be to take a circumventing path. Heading toward the spot where the crash barrier ends and then making our way along the island's eastern perimeter.

The maneuver will allow us to get within hearing range without having to undertake the arduous effort of trying to cut through the crowd directly.

However sensible the move, it will still take a good deal of energy. And the question arises, once again, of whether the expenditure will be worth it.

Sometimes you do need to stop and think a moment, take time to consider the matter a little more deeply before blindly forging on. We might undertake the effort to get closer to the spokesman, only to find that he still could not be heard. The achievement questionable, the sense of fulfillment deferred.

He could be pantomiming the delivery, for all we know. His words could mean little, his true audience not us.

What is it that we expect to hear anyway. What is it that we expect to gain.

Crowd analytics help shed light on the issue. Information about movements and physiological states drawn from the Ambler's extensor. This reveals an audience in a state of receptivity and involvement that correlates with hearing, at least in the lower portion of the island. Suggesting that the likelihood of receiving and reacting to the spokesman's voice starts to increase just past the midpoint. The probability increases as you advance further from there. Those clustered in the immediate range of the speaker display conclusive signs of auditory excitation, even seem to be roiling in a surplus of it. Their expressions are so vigorous and unrestrained as to appear frenzied, awash in an overabundance of stimulation that is striking in its contrast to the conditions at this end.

I imagine them capable of morphic variation. Able to transmute, become permeable, disseminated and aggregated anew.

I can feel the analyses laying the groundwork for proceeding. Contouring the space of possibility, setting the stage for the engagement in time. Moving from ideas to built paths, symbols to infrastructure. Negotiating the terms of progression, the rhythms of operation. Merging, overlaying. Stopping and advancing. Isolating details and then motoring continuity between the points located, the elements pinpointed in the instance.

They say that you need a model of reality to navigate that reality. But reality needs the model even more. It is the model that sustains it, draws form out.

We have hardly taken two steps when someone in a broad-shouldered frock coat lurches toward us, as if thrown by an overwhelming force.

I noticed this person earlier, tugging at someone's arm and casting a disparaging look our way. I paid her no mind, I have quite gotten used to it. The Ambler tends to awaken complicated feelings in others, arousing sympathy but also very often ill-will. As if it embodied something they would rather not face, portended some condition they would rather not accept.

Words, in being spoken, elicit proximity, strive for correspondence, but the look, it withholds, works the edge.

It is always a challenge to anticipate the movements of unaided foot travelers, no matter how advanced the predictive capability. The range of possible movements is less circumscribed, the intentions cloudy, the decisions rash.

Some say that the inner workings of artificial agents are too inscrutable. But trying to decipher the rationales of real people is not any easier. Making sense of what they are trying to do. What they are expecting to find. What has driven them to make a particular decision, what they are trying to accomplish or why.

The traveler in the frock coat keeps her eyes fixed straight ahead on the speaker in the distance, maintaining a rapt expression, as if she were awestruck by the spokesman's oratory, even though there is no possible way she could be hearing it. All it is possible to hear at this range are the back and forth shouts of people requesting clarification, imploring others to repeat what the speaker has said, relay what they have not heard or confirm what they think he did say. Any remaining possibility that the spokesman could actually be heard is drowned out by this clamor, and while some near the front have tried to help out by shouting lines of his dialogue back, others have shouted their own lines, whether as corrective or riposte. Making it difficult to know how to gauge these transmitted phrases, whether they are coming or going, so to speak.

The roar of a passing tanker causes the crowd to reel sideward, freeing up a space along the curb into which a cluster of newcomers pour.

I recognize the three colleagues who arrived just after us, camera gear in tow.

Hello, I shout, waving.

We almost make it to the curb when the leg sensors detect something moving underfoot, causing us to rear up in anticipation. The Ambler is highly attuned to ground variances, the jointed nature of the limbed units allows increased obstacle-surmounting capacity, ambulatory fluency and speed. It can wade through floods, scrabble across rocks, clamber up hillsides. But there are some instances that are too extraordinary to accommodate without interruption.

The undercarriage light flicks on to reveal a small person, advancing along the pavement on all fours. The man can hardly be seen amid the thick canopy of bodies, not even by his companion, outfitted in a metal carapace that elevates the arms, juts the elbows and forces the chin up.

In the distance the spokesman can be seen lifting a forefinger and pausing, as if the crowd had missed a subtle distinction. He allows a moment to pass, then swings his arms upward with such fervency it causes the assembly to recoil, momentarily destabilizing its cohesiveness.

The crowd swings back, restoring unity.

The speaker flutters his uplifted hands, then stares at the fingers of each hand, one after the other, as if surprised to find them there.

Behind him, the two converging avenues that the island interleaves, together with the third entering from the west, meld into the higher-order thoroughfare that roars onward, funneling the cavalcade of vehicles onto the highways that sweep onward from there.

The elongations of concrete lanes, the swirling cues of exits. The crisscrosses of flyovers, the gridded arrays of parking lots, the scribbles of side streets, the meanderings of frontage roads. Overlaps and differentials, interchanges and swivels, underflows and loopbacks. Concurrency of pathway and phrase, route and routine.

Experience generalizing in forms that allow retreading. Variation, repetition, paraphrasing.

A traffic-tossed figure in a helmet has been trying to push his way over, all but knocking down an elder who grabs him by the arm, trying to hold him back.

A group of attendees advances in the wake, taking the opportunity to improve its vantage points.

What is it that you expect to find. What is ahead for you now.

We have made it to the perimeter and can progress more steadily now. Having one set of legs on each side of the curb allows us to maintain balance, avoid the kind of side-to-side sway that otherwise happens with a biped while, at the same time, retain the dexterity to avoid hindrances, maneuver around obstacles, roll with the give-and-take of the crowd.

Action gets afforded, more or less securely, from the hold. Everything is poised among forces applied and resisted. Held more or less stably, more or less firmly.

Someone in a green tracksuit has elbowed his way over, twisting away from a huddle of attendees that has been trying to block him from passing. Unsure of their place, yet loath to surrender it.

A delivery pod whisks by, but in the wrong direction. It prompts us to draw in—a slight contrapposto.

We can see the speaker a little more clearly now that we have passed the halfway mark. He points westward to the connecting flyover, then to the interchange, then back to the flyover. We join the audience glancing mechanically back and forth.

The elaborate feat of infrastructural engineering supports the effort, connects the indicators, brings awareness into line. Consolidates the flows, streamlines the affect, contours the volume.

His stage has been constructed atop the point where the island narrows to a V. It has been arranged to exploit the dramatic backdrop, obviously. Leaving the cameras no choice as to the framing.

We zoom in for a closer look.

The spokesman gazes wide-eyed and open-mouthed at the crowd, then shoots his arms skyward, palms out, fingertips flexing. The crowd in his vicinity erupts, as if rejoicing. Awash in a surplus of euphoria and aggression, accordance and strife.

Noses are thumbed, fists shaken in the air. Ripples of dissatisfaction flare.

The speaker points eastward to the construction site of the new highway, then pivots toward the interchange in a broad, overarching sweep.

A group of enthusiasts makes headbanging gestures, signaling appreciation of the performance.

The percussive whump of construction machinery adds an underscoring pulse, as if the relentless labor of infrastructure building were keeping time, laying the groundwork for the proceeding.

We zoom in and out, scale up and down, switch from abstract maps to situated views, landscape to detail.

We diagram the architecture, observe from abstraction. Model the scene of which the speaker is part. Transform the island into a machine for directing attention. Speculate about why the site was chosen and the presentation organized this way. Consider that it provides both scenographic advantage and inherent regulatory potential. The prospect of having a spectacular background for the news coverage while having crowd control functions built in. An infrastructure that can perform itself as spectacle while at the same time, regulate the conditions of experiencing it.

The speaker escalates his oratory as the crowd whirls, cheering and booing amid the haze. Thumbs are raised in affirmation, hands rubbed in expectation.

An enthusiast pushes her way over to us, holds up a handlike effector and gives us a sly, knowing smile.

The gripper is much easier to control than a five-fingered hand, she says, reaching out and touching me gently on the arm.

As we approach the vicinity where the speaker is standing, we can hear him beseeching the crowd to fear not. He hurls his arms upward again with great vigor and then sets forth with a series of exhortations, each accented with a corresponding move. Expressions that seem less concerned with the delivering of content than establishing the parameters within which it will flow. The contours of progression, the structures of operation. The conditions of passage, the rhythms of phrasing. Intervals of isolating and motoring. Locating and continuing.

The speaker steps off his platform and makes a welcoming gesture, like a host ushering the headline attraction onto the stage.

We can detect a cylindrical apparatus installed on the platform behind him. The platform he has been standing on is not merely a stage—he and the apparatus are both there to serve it, facilitate intake, draw upon available force. Convert the onrush of traffic to energy. Channel transmission, conduct transfer and aggregation. Enable conveyance and then disappear, dissolve into the substructure of the enabling.

A celebrant is pushing through the group from behind, yielding to the impulse to see. He brushes past, then swings round and freezes upon catching sight of us. His eyes widen, his face grows pale and he emits a piercing screech—an unsparing current of pure sound that seems to cut through the hubbub, momentarily disable time.

It is highly unusual for a grown person to produce sound in that register.

Our sound-cancelling countermeasure spouts fast, like an airbag.

A momentary silence falls across the crowd.

Hello, I say, waving.

There are always potentials to realize, even in a space like this, a mere interlude, interstice amid the flows. Always the chance of encountering a breakthrough, always the chance of discovering the one thing that could change everything.

You can forge ahead without giving the matter much thought in these instances or you can stop to think for a moment before making the expenditure, stop to consider how often it is that you have gone to the trouble to get somewhere, only to find yourself questioning, upon the arrival, whether the effort was worth it. The accomplishment illusory. The sense of fulfillment deferred.

You can try to get a deeper sense of what had led you to set out so blindly on those occasions, consider what it was that you were expecting to find. The question of what drove you. Those incentives for moving, inducements for pulling. What they were all about.

If you try to approach the question thoroughly, gain a profound sense of the truth, then it must be illumined by another light, it must come to you outside your experiential purview. It requires a broader field of past experience to sift through, a larger set of historical data to gauge. A realm of ability that is not individualized, yet is somehow actualized, informed in the life of character. Embedded in machineries that compose actors. Differentiated aspects that are usually incorporated into a coherent whole, but which, when examined more closely, extend outward, connect to vehicles that assist performance, faculties that extend competence. Narratives that lend continuity, routines that lend coherency.

You might wonder whether you are really any longer the same person. Whether you are really any longer the same person driven in the same way.

21

Free Industrial Corridor

The vehicles aligned on the tarmac of the test site, immaculately buffed by the effects team, appear opaque and featureless under the shimmering light of the afternoon sun, now approaching the golden hour, that fleeting period when colors become warmer, shadows less harsh.

Positioning them on the runway of a test facility has imbued them with the tenor of the aeronautic, suggesting that the host company, a defense contractor specializing in aerospace, has extended its operations to land. Couching the harsh reality of conquest in the normalized experience of motoring. Replacing the somber reality of transit with the seductions of ascendance. Embedding the military in the domestic, orienting the civilian toward the sky.

Industrial Highway

The chairman has been doing his best to stay focused. Trying not to think about the lack of space. Trying not to think about the growing crush of bodies in the car. Trying to keep his mind on the speech, concentrate on the points he is to make in his statements. Time constraints usually work in his favor, help keep him focused, help ward off his lingering unease, but the oppressive atmosphere of the cabin undermines these efforts, the feeling of confinement threatens to pull him off track, inflame his misgivings, allow his deep-seated worries to rise up anew. His distaste for appearances, his fear of contact, his aversion to crowds.

He should have listened to his gut instincts and gotten out of this engagement. Right away this morning, while he had the chance.

One must pay heed to what the circumstance is telling you, listen to what the circumstance forebodes—this, one of the little truisms from the life enhancement program that he usually runs before breakfast, a sunrise session of guided visualization training and transformational breath work, but which he was unable to run this morning because of the problems he had to contend with straightaway.

He felt feverish when he woke up, considered that he might be afflicted with something, decided he probably was and sat spellbound on the toilet for a long while after spending an hour combing through the carpet on his hands and knees to find the pills he had knocked from the counter while trying to activate the earpiece. The earpiece works well enough, but has been picking up the wrong signal at times, which is worrisome.

He is wholly unprepared for this speech, there is no doubt about it. There is hardly any time to finish the talking points let alone memorize them, as he always takes great pains to do.

He has never been one to take the easy way out, has always been determined to avoid using the earpiece as a replacement for faculties he himself should be exercising. He uses it only for rehearsal, never for the presentation itself. A tool for the practice not the performance.

The speech before the last, or maybe three or four speeches ago, hard to remember when, he did allow himself to skip the first few rounds of the memorization process and let the device prompt him with the first few words of each line. But he remembered the bulk of the speech, needed only the line prompts to be able to complete the sentence, perform the line with an expressive flourish commensurate to its weight. A minimal line prompt was all that was necessary to bring the content into play, intone the phrase after the voice of the trainer faded away.

He does not want to do that again, does not want to make that a habit, does not want to allow his own faculty of memory to weaken in the least. If you rely too much on a tool like that you are putting your own competence on the line. There is always the chance that the transmission can be disrupted, the signal lost, the support rescinded and you are left standing there like an idiot, unable to remember what comes next. It happened to him once, four or five speeches ago, maybe more recently, hard to remember exactly when but the feeling is still fresh, the memory sharp enough to call to mind the humiliation.

He will never again let that happen, will never again put himself in that position.

Besides, the memorization process itself has many advantages—the practice itself benefits you in the long run no matter how it is applied. It helps sharpen the mind, elevate competency, lend sensory acuity. The life enhancement program has helped him appreciate the value of practice for its own sake.

Its potential not only to improve capability but to regulate surplus energy, restrain compulsions. Instill the discipline needed to ward off preoccupations, minimize adverse thoughts. It helps subdue that inner voice that always gravitates toward the worst, helps manage those compulsions that cannot be fully controlled, only quieted.

The point is not to eliminate the negative thoughts, but to prevent them from becoming worries. Overwrite the cycles of harmful behavior to which they are bound. Supplant them with new regimens, cycles of increase that counteract the inertial pull of habit.

There are times when it is better to overwrite the codes, reprogram the program rather than try to do away with it entirely. The program is going to be there anyway.

The deep breathing exercises he has been performing have inspired him to try taking another dose of decongestant from the inhaler. He suspects that none of the medication was released from the canister when he first used it a short time ago, even though he is quite confident he performed the discharge correctly—inhaling deeply as he pressed the little plastic mouthpiece and then holding his breath for the required ten seconds before releasing the aerosol. He suspects it contained nothing but propellant.

He is unable to raise the hand in which the canister is held at the moment because of the mammoth makeup box that Hair and Makeup have placed on the seat next to him. The box has pinned the lower part of the apron beneath it and stretched the rubbery fabric crosswise across the forearm. The airspace above it is filled with racks of cantilevered trays. The kind that swing outward and upward from the bottom compartment in tiers.

The little pressurized canister rattles against the underside, making a clattering noise.

When you are preparing a speech it is essential to find the right movements, allow gestures to flow naturally from the words, allow them to shape one another, allow voice and mannerism to coincide. An effective speaker must allow physical expression, must allow thought to animate action. You are not just a talking head—you must rehearse bodily too. To know is to know how to move.

He thinks about trying to snatch the arm out in one swift yank, but such an act has an air of desperation about it, not the quality of temperance he seeks.

One must aspire to an awareness free of grasping, free of habitual cycles of need.

The junior safety engineer in the front seat turns around and casts him a concerned look, or a look that expresses something like concern, hard to tell exactly because of the headgear he is wearing, which has a mouth-slot that curves upward at both ends, suggesting enjoyment, even as the features as a whole remain unreadable.

Talk to the hand, is how he wants to respond, extending the free arm and wiggling the grippers. But after his accident on the stairwell that morning he has been having problems getting the limb to work properly. It is all he can do to manipulate the paddle mirror he grips in the handlike extremity right now.

There is a lag between the decision to move and the movement that follows. Or rather, between the action and the decision that justifies it retrospectively.

Ideas are not shaped in advance of the movement. Ideas are shaped by the way you move.

He is not too worried about the problem—he is grateful that he has an arm to wield at all. The process of learning how to use it has given him a fresh perspective on life. He has come to appreciate the value of challenges, how they revitalize your capacity for learning. The value of setbacks, how they bring renewed gratitude for what you have.

That a simple thought can be translated into movement so seamlessly, orchestrated in a way that mimics the way your body would naturally move, even though the thought mechanisms that cause an arm to act are still not fully understood—this is nothing short of miraculous.

One should never take anything for granted. Each time you reach for something could be the last. A grip can relinquish its object and vanish in an instant. Like your lap when you stand up. It is nothing outside the act of its doing. Not a possession but an availability.

There is no time for indulging these thoughts, they are not the kind of refrains he needs to be concentrating on, not the kind of points he needs to determine for the talk. He needs to keep himself focused on the people he actually has to attend to, the audience he has to address, the various dissenters he has to anticipate in the speech. The traffic neutrality activists. Driver Coalitionists. Advocates of human-centric autonomy. People Persons. They will be waiting on the tarmac, ready to heckle. It takes a lot of concentration to understand their mindsets, find the best way to counter their views without losing stride. Circumvent their habitual reactions, steer them away from the idea that the command cabin is a stronghold worth defending. That the tasks of operation are truly in their hands. That the driver they speak of can defy the imperatives of automation, stand firm against the inevitability of deposing.

He should have listened to his intuition and bailed out of the whole thing. He is hardly ready. There is little time left to hone the catchlines let alone memorize them, inhabit their structure, internalize their rhythms.

It is not only the packed cabin that makes it so difficult but the tightness of the apron, especially the neckband, tethered to the headrest to prevent the head from lopping as Hair and Makeup, outfitted in a great billowing cloak lined with fur, bear down upon him with diligence.

He tries to glance sideways to see who is there, for he is never quite certain who has shown up, whether it is two persons, one doing hair, the other makeup, or one person doing both. Those playing the roles always seem to be more or less coincident with the roles being played, always combined within a single outfit that remains constant no matter who makes it up.

To be an effective presenter you must know how to move, you must allow physical expression, must allow thought to animate action. Otherwise the body gets relegated to a subordinate role, as if it were merely a puppet, and when it comes time for the performance, you discover that it does not have the fluidity you expect. The presentation seems forced and overly contrived, the delivery heavy-handed rather than nimble. You have to manufacture a false sense of confidence that the audience can detect.

The ability to make the strenuous seem easy is essential to achieving a quality of gracefulness, the highest of the virtues one can aspire to. It always comes without fanfare and always seems fluent, never calling attention to the labor required to reach it, the great care and perseverance demanded for it to be attained.

He had been unable to finish the rehearsal on the last speech, but was able to justify this because at least he remembered the important part, did not need to have the training-agent feed him every line. Or maybe he did, it is hard to remember exactly because there are times when the agent's off-stage voice, which is designed to sound like you, reflect your vocal characteristics, mimic cadence and tone, gets a little too close to your own. It has the quality of being immediately and transparently there, present in itself, complete without need of reflection. Separate and a part of you, singular and paired.

For the last speech, he did end up ceding some of the composition work to the algorithm, but wrote most of it himself. A good part of it at least. How much exactly is hard to say, because the suggestions made by the program turn out to be fairly accurate, sound like something you really would say, or did say.

He has always been inclined to consider his speech as a personal expression of his original thought, but lately he has come to wonder. Considering how accurately the system is able to predict his intentions, have a better idea than he does of where he is headed, where his thoughts are headed.

The farther out from the original idea you go, the less accurate the prediction. But it is easy to forget where the original was.

A metal armature on the far end is knocking against the windowpane with a rhythmic intensity, like exclamation. A technician is rummaging under the seat in that area, effecting kinetic changes all the way up.

He has been trying to maneuver the paddle mirror into the right position for monitoring the cosmetic progress, but Hair and Makeup, currently applying foundation with great vigor, have bent down so close to him that he can hardly see his reflection at all. The portions of himself he is able to catch sight of here and there have each caused an involuntary spasm of abhorrence. Not only because of his own pained reflection, but because of the enormous obtruding fingers, thick and stained at the ends, that press upon him at the same time.

High concentrations of microbes can be found on bare hands even more than on the bristled and padded instruments that would otherwise be used for this purpose. Not to mention the containers and trays where pathogens lay in wait, ready to hitchhike, like malicious intruders on an update.

Likewise with handles, lids, touch displays, and knobs.

The carrier bins of the mammoth makeup box. The rack handles, bonnets, and locking lips on the little receptacles.

The great billowing cloak worn by Hair and Makeup, stained with solvent, sweeps across the cabin in broad strokes, whipping up particulate, clouding the air. Adorned with dust ruffles, ribbons, and straps that fall every which way, making it difficult to track where the various extremities are placed as they shuttle among the contact points of the cabin interior. Stopping and starting, bending and elongating, coming into being as they move through time. An occasional thump against the sidewall, like punctuation.

He once thought that behind every surface lurked the possibility of a horror. But the true horror is right there on top.

Public appearances always bring out the worst in him, cause him to fixate on the foulest kinds of pathogenic dreads. Not only the routes of direct contact with the skin, the kind easiest to visualize, but the airborne pathways that elude detection and the most insidious of all, the fecal-oral.

That is why he always takes his own car, a Dominion model designed to minimize attack surface area, supply prophylactic provision. Even though the red team has detained it he could have arranged for a substitute in the meantime. At least until the penetration tests are run. He could have arranged for a comparable model like a Marga or one of the higher priced trim levels. A Renunciant, an Exodus. Or a NO.

Why had he not done that? Refused to take a shared car, demanded a NO, or bailed out of the whole thing. The cars run by the fleets are not well maintained, they have too many unsecured openings, you can never be sure of how well they have been disinfected and who has been in them before you. They do not make the cleaning logs public, do not disclose whether they use antimicrobial sprayers, electrostatic foggers or robotic scrubbers. They tell you they use hospital-grade disinfectants, spray the employees between jobs and impose a waiting period between bookings but you can never be sure who has been in there or when. The surfaces are greasy, the panels smudged, the fabric stained. The air is distinctly feculent.

He has found dried mucus, pubic hair, clotted rags. Even a tooth.

He once opened the door of a fleet-run citycar and a lump of fat fell out, ruining his shoes. He had spent the whole of that morning scrambling for something to wear, had scarcely been able to pull together any sort of look and after that incident, had to start the whole process over again.

Another time, he boarded a top of the line Spectrafleet, the Ego Plus, which has a military-grade air filtration system, contact-free surfaces and self-cleaning seats, and while he was inspecting the footwell, came upon an elfin character—a stowaway—peering out at him.

With every calamity comes an advancement, ready to shine forth. With every drawback, a prospect of renewal.

The involuntary reactions he has been experiencing have resulted in considerable smudging and spillover, with much of the powder making its way into his hair, which remains in bad shape, admittedly, after it was forcibly blown dry when he had to stick his head out the window to vomit on the way over. Providing a sobering reminder of how little remains.

The more aerodynamic the car, the more forceful and turbulent the wind buffeting—this, an unfortunate effect.

Has he brought this upon himself somehow, he cannot help but wonder sometimes. Not intentionally, but by means of some unconscious impulse that the limb picks up on. Or by means of some nonconscious impulse that is not really his, but which is channeled through him and acted upon anyway. Expressing what is not acted out knowingly, expressing that which acts through him less willingly.

He should have listened to his intuition and gotten out of this engagement. Should have been alert to what the situation portended, listened to his inner voice and bailed.

One must learn to receive experience on its own terms. The most unpleasant situations can be the strongest sources of knowledge. The aspects we think of as negative the impetus for learning and growth.

He is gnashing his teeth just thinking about it.

The technician in the front seat, who he has been trying to get rid of, is clawing at the dashboard and grunting. Murmuring something unintelligible into the driveline.

Out with it! is what he wants to say to him, giving a whack against his seat back with the paddle mirror.

But he cannot say anything, can hardly even clear his throat at the moment with Hair and Makeup pressing upon the corners of the mouth, prompting him to keep it open so that the teeth, badly discolored, can be dabbed with resin. The clenching and grinding habits have given rise to a particularly grim state of affairs in there.

One must aspire to a life free of conditioned patterns, free of habitual cycles of grinding.

A buccal retractor has been inserted to keep the orifice stretched, the gums bared. The neckband of the apron tightened more securely to the headrest to minimize droop.

Restraints are not there to curb freedom, but to teach and reveal.

Strands of saliva are removed with a suction device. The tongue is pushed back with a depressor. The lips, thin and pale, outlined with color.

He pushes into the prophylactic seat cover for reassurance.

Within every horror lurks an enticement, ready to shine forth. With every aversion, the prospect of renewal.

One must affirm the rigors of the discipline, learn to restrain the affects, subdue the low-level anxieties that otherwise gain hold. If the engine of the rehearsal is not running smoothly it gives rise to unhealthy preoccupations, strengthens deep-seated aversions. Feelings of impending catastrophe that, deprived of the momentum that will curb them, rise up to fill the void.

Test Drive

A minipod crashed through the window of the Driveline facility. It lodged between the side jambs and remained there, nose cone poking out over the mezzanine. The entire building emptied out in a matter of seconds. I had never seen people move that fast on foot—certainly not the people there, who hardly ever strayed from their stations. The space has an open, hangar-style design in order to increase cross-team camaraderie and collaboration, but it did not have that effect at all, at least from what I could see. What it did seem to increase was cortisol.

The fact that I remained inside the building prompted me to remark, as in a stage whisper, *she remained inside*. One of those heightened moments when, without even being aware of it, I will begin to note the situation in detail, sketch out the scene more explicitly, write myself into it with greater clarity. And this observer who until that moment had had a character role will now also be standing in the wings, will now be both conveyor and conveyed, will now inhabit two different registers, become a little bit more than before.

The pod was quickly removed. They never did find out who or what was inside it, they only knew that the payload, whatever it was, had been ejected before impact.

The floor was cleared, the broken window patched up, exterior forces walled off again. Everyone went back to their stations, returned to the simulated worlds of the highways where experience could be gained much more manageably. Contingencies worked through, obstacles confronted, prototypes tested without threat of reality intervening. Dangerous scenarios played out before they happen, diminishing their potential to alarm.

I assumed that everything would return to normal, or what I took to be normal since I had not really been there long enough to know. But the episode seemed to affect the way others treated me, as if I were somehow responsible. Vague signs of unease, like giving me a wide berth whenever I passed.

The supervisor, who had until then been accommodating of my ambulatory difficulties, more or less, began to gesture toward me while rapping her arm against the wall, an act that I saw her perform repeatedly, to no discernible end. As if she were trying to convey some idea while at the same time trying to divest the act of symbolic function.

I knew it was time to move on.

22

Eastern Corridor

Heading east along the Crosstown, thinking about the contours of the world that the algorithms model. The texture of involvement. The experience beneath the account.

A car is moving alongside me in the adjoining lane—a Compiler, same model and type. It is moving at exactly the same speed, making it seem as if a corridor has been opened between us, a zone of stillness that cuts laterally across the onward rush of traffic. The confluence of car windows holds us in profile, immobilizes us like images within the sidelong scope of the overlaid frames.

A sidelong theater. A machinery of staging, of energy holding, compressing and stilling. A theater where the car performs the passenger, brings the surrounding choreography to the fore. An automotive staging. A machinery of staging that cuts through the artifice of the frame.

We are riding side by side, connected in a way that does not require us to address one another, pose questions about the performance in which we are joined. The explanation, if there is one, is to be gotten at indirectly, in the lateral correspondence not the colloquy.

The cars ahead of us are pulling over to the edge of the highway, as if clearing the way for a motorcade to pass through.

We are the motorcade.

Overdrive

In the event of a system failure, the Overdrive must be able to assume the driving functions as surely as if it were present in the cabin along with you. It must be able to act through the vehicle, inhabit the driver's role.

You do not want to get in the way if this happens—you want to open yourself to what comes, allow yourself to be swept up, held from without. Attune to what is provided you. Affirm the pathway, accept the awareness, give way to the informing expression. Know that the best possible response is being drawn through you. That another layer of action coincides with yours, extends the range of your ability, taps into wider channels of expressing.

Think of those moments when you feel at one with the machine, your sense of self retracting and expanding in accordance with the ebbs and flows of traffic. Moments when you channel the impulse, allow what is there. Subordinate the drive, consolidate the direction, summon the will. Tap into the affirmation at the basis. Scale to those levels where you are inherent. As if you were inside the driving, inside the thinking, inside the acting. Inside the operation that acts. Embodied in the role you are playing but at the same time disassociated from it, inhabiting some larger strata of enunciation, some larger domain of composition where the boundaries are not so readily apparent, the terms not so availably drawn. Channeling the informing without need of presumptions that will cause unnecessary limitation, stir up undue interference.

By way of these extraordinary encounters the novel act is synthesized. The backup kicks in, the system trains, the car learns how to handle the situation without need of assistance the next time around. The number of interventions decreases as the system improves. The responsibilities consolidate into fewer and fewer hands. The expertise integrates into more and more cars.

Functions reorganize, roles readjust. Forms are dispatched and reassembled over points in space and time. Operators tasked with emergency calls help assuage the fears of those on the line. Auto Assists tasked with service responsibilities function as counselors of sorts.

In their capacities as analysts and confidantes, advisors and trainers, the Overdrive agents are already called to act in this manner, summoned to address that most basic of human needs, the urge to share an affinity, develop a sense of parity and rapport. Even those who would otherwise forego contact tend to reach out in exceptional circumstances when the demand for an answer overwhelms. That kind of intimate connection that only a shared catastrophe can bring, when we overcome the differences that normally keep us apart.

Is not the essence of listening the ability to come out of yourself, lose your self-preoccupation and reside with someone else, in such a way as to expand the space of the present? Form a disseminated mode of intimacy, a zone of proximity that is abundant, a closeness that is excessive and full.

The unformed nature of the Overdrives accords them an uncanny ability to experience the world outside the limits of selfhood while conforming to the requirements of social relation. An ability to enter the life of the driver, reflect their desires, elicit ideas while maintaining parity, relative normalcy and similarity. An ability to serve as a counterpart who is not fully embodied as an other, indeterminate as a voice of conscience but nonetheless very real. Attuned to the vagaries of sensation, resolved to forms commensurate with your own. Forms that mirror your nature, ensure recognizability, ensure that you figure centrally.

23

The Gyre

A sky-gray Compiler turns onto the service road, headlights glaring, and makes a beeline toward the cycloidal structure at the terminus. A facility designed to ensure an environment free of radio frequency interference, shield the complex from electromagnetic radiation that can disrupt the sensitive measurements of the apparatus inside.

A ban on radio-based communication extends to the surrounding area. Which the Compiler has just defied.

To detect and intercept without telematics, a formidable mission: such is the task of the sentries who roam the grounds on horseback in rotating shifts, spot-checking vehicles, hunting down rogue signals, confiscating devices, and detaining perpetrators without benefit of those tools that would greatly aid their facility, boost their capacity to outwit opponents, coordinate action, conduct systemic intensification. Their antiquated assembly of optical instruments and monitoring techniques is all but useless in the presence of infiltrators far better equipped. Denied the virtues of data aggregated, maps updated, behaviors modeled, they are forced to engage the terrain as a realm with its own unique material considerations, not just as a landscape of movements to track but of innumerable practices to comprehend, unrelenting procedures of energy conversion and matter transformation—procuring and managing resources in untold compromises and tradeoffs. All the while striving to preserve dominion, sustain mastery, maintain the upper hand.

It goes without saying, then, that the watchman now on duty, as with his teammates, needs all the help he can get. While his perceptual skill is duly noted by his fellow officers, it will hardly elicit their admiration, will hardly warrant their praise: in their view, it is far too cerebral for the mission, all too often simply distracts, causes unnecessary obfuscation, emphasizes deliberation rather than act. Encumbered as it is by those tattered old volumes, extraneously loaded in his saddlebag, upon whose margins he chronicles his rounds—volumes whose true nature he takes great care to conceal, for unbeknownst to these fellow officers, they are actually publications, literary ones at that: fiction overlaid with fact. Books of the romance genre, to be precise, that storied variety based on the ineluctability of the heroic quest, the disciplined, noble search for a love that is passionate and principled, virtuous and in some measure illicit. Gallant tales of intrepid and valorous acts, oriented toward ideals of courtliness that his teammates would surely mock, but which, to him, remain evermore relevant to the present day. Not necessarily in terms of the stories themselves but in the machinery that drives them, the codes that govern them, the ethical principles that can be absorbed through conscientious study and practice, assimilated from those who, in their timeless wisdom, have helped pave the way. It is the kind of informing that comes through language but is much more than that, and which, through the concerted effort of attuning to it, ingraining it in conduct, can be accessed when the time comes, brought to bear on the situation at hand.

Among all these works, none have served him better than the present one, the one he has currently at the ready, the work upon whose pages is inscribed the life he himself could have lived; the sentences he could well have composed; the love that, should fate have wished it so, could have been his.

He has been on rounds all night, this valiant watchman, moving among the various vantage points he occupies routinely on the circuit. Trotting among the hilltops and valleys on his loyal steed, traversing the viaducts and bluffs at regular intervals on his mount. Alternating between surveying, inscribing, and reading at each stop. At times allowing thoughts to cross the threshold of expression, muffled by the visored helmet that he seldom removes and does not remove now, even as he alights—the very moment that the aforementioned Compiler races by him along the foothill, eluding detection.

Between paper and scene, instrument and mind; jumping ahead in position, looping back in time: the passages he adds make it easy for him to veer off, weave back and forth among the chronicles of old and new, the events experienced and the acts conveyed in words. The figure on the quest—he is shaped in the relays, composed within the overlapping stage.

Indeed he could have written this quest, could have written any scene amid the interplay, recorded any or all of them on the stage of action taking shape.

But look! The infiltrating Compiler is about to be caught, in flagrante, by the watchman's unofficial aides-de-camp—a throng of foil-clad electrosensitives who come upon it in a flourish. Their numbers are all but indeterminable beneath the clusters of buckling silver veneer, glimmering under the lights of the burning torches, which sway indiscriminately above the crinkle. Heads peer out amid the billowing mass; here a leg shuffles, there a foot shakes, there an arm flails as if to gather up the composite and express with its whole being an urge, motor a meaning, whip up the energetic clamor on which the group could thrive.

The beams of the slowing Compiler shine upon it, help bring its constituents into view.

Of this undercover community, little is acknowledged in the records. The support that it provides cannot be sanctioned, even though the security teams have come to depend on it, lacking as they do the resources to cover the territory fully. Especially those overlooked hollows, desolate burrows and gullies, grim boreholes and nooks with which the electrosensitives are intimately familiar, and from which they might suddenly spring forth, clad in protective aluminum wrap, to set upon transgressors with fervor.

Churning under, in ways too cumbersome and slow to captivate the eye; plodding along, bereft of the overview that moves at the speed of light, resolves infrastructure to surface, process to form.

They come from all walks of life, these lay practitioners, drawn to the area to partake of the electromagnetic silence for their own purposes, operating in accordance with suppositions that, unlike those of the researchers who work inside the Gyre, lie beyond the scope of scientific understanding. For them, the area's diminishment of electromagnetic radiation is thought to offer benefits both physical and mental. Lessening the pathological symptoms of environmental intolerance, instilling clarity of perception and boosting telepathic potential.

Although the functions of the apparatus they help protect are largely incomprehensible to them—as opaque and impenetrable as the building in which it is housed—they do experience an affinity with it; a kind of fondness, even. They share its extreme sensitivity, for their own sensory and cognitive capacities are likewise disrupted by unwanted signals. The bond goes only so far, however, for they remain suspicious of the methods it deploys and the truths it reveals, opting to pursue their own path to enlightenment, however unsupportable the tenets. The absence of mobile devices, the mandatory disabling of onboard automotive connectivity and the ban on radar and broadcasting, even for the vehicles that fly overhead, clears the air for alternative orders of communicative experience, however inclined toward the terrestrial or otherworldly.

The valorous watchman is already on the move, alerted by the shower of diffused light generated by the Compiler's highbeams as they bounce off the nebulous foil mass undulating in the street before it. Suspended in the currents, buoyed by the charge. Features coalescing and unfolding in the striving, fluctuating like membranes in the dance. Reinforcing, reaching. Forming in proceeding.

He gallops toward the scene with finesse, lance held high, helmet bobbing, grin wide, teeth bared and protruding—rushing down the hillside toward that point where, upon the road, is staged that indecipherable scene, shapeless and incomplete, whose apprehension he will nobly claim. That fledgling infraction, as vague and indeterminate as he, the valiant sentry who has it in his sights—the fearless defender who has now entered the stage of action, crossed that point of no return, reached that point when he is no longer inscribed in any one passage, that stage where all that had defined him has changed.

He bursts gallantly upon the scene as the throng of electrosensitives scurries down the hillside, scattering as fast as it came. Contours inscrutable, absorbed in the repertoire of attributes, the reservoir of properties to mine. Offerings, drawbacks. Negotiating passageways for continuance, segueing in and out of paths. Entering, cohering. Forming in maneuvering.

One solitary figure has been left behind, marooned upon the blacktop, unplugged from the throng, secured only by a helmet of foil. Arms flung out, gazing wide-eyed at the Compiler, immobilized by the harsh, dreamlike glare of its lights.

The watchman draws closer, lifts his visor and ejaculates:

Flee not!

He then cues his hard-hoofed stallion to turn toward the offending coach, squaring his shoulders and hips, applying pressure to the inside stirrup with one leg while tapping to the girth with the other, thus displaying his talent: he who strives to transform the ordinary into the noble, remedy the inherent deception of form.

He advances with an abrupt lurch upon concluding the move and then, with reins tightly gripped, gallantly rears skyward to elevate the authority of his command that he delivers forthwith—the demand that the infiltrator submit, relinquish the payload, divulge what lay within.

The offending coach, despite the exigency of the order, discloses naught.

No states to detect, no movements to gauge. No driver to address, no victory to claim.

Nothing to be reached, sensed, defined, said.

The effort to probe, hustled to the outside instead.

Author Biography

Jordan Crandall is Professor of Visual Arts at University of California, San Diego. He is the author of five books, including *Drive*, an anthology of his artworks, media installations, and theoretical writings published by Neue Galerie Graz and ZKM Center for Art and Media Karlsruhe. In 2011 he was the recipient of the Vilém Flusser Theory Award for outstanding research in media art and digital culture. *Autodrive* is his first work of fiction.